THE MYSTERY OF RUBY'S SUGAR

ROSE DONOVAN

Moon Snail Press

MORE RUBY DOVE MYSTERIES

Sign up for updates and bonus material. Details can be found at the end of *The Mystery of Ruby's Sugar*.

Cast of Characters at Pauncefort Hall

Ruby Dove – Student of chemistry at Oxford, fashion designer and amateur spy-sleuth. On a mission to avenge her family.

Fina Aubrey-Havelock – Student of history at Oxford, assistant seamstress to Ruby and her best friend. Also warming to the spy-sleuth role.

Alma, Countess of Snittlegarth (Lady Snittlegarth) – Wife of Roger, lover of tropical fish. Aunt to Charlotte, Edgar and Granville.

Roger, Earl of Snittlegarth (Lord Snittlegarth) – Husband of Alma, lover of the Yuletide season. Uncle to Charlotte, Edgar and Granville.

Charlotte Sykes-Duckworth – Daughter of Henry Sykes-Duckworth, Earl of Malvern. Niece of Alma and Roger. Keeper of Pauncefort Hall.

Granville Sykes-Duckworth – Elder son of Henry Sykes-Duckworth, Earl of Malvern. Nephew of Alma and Roger. Lover of fascism. Set to take the reins of the family's sugar empire.

Edgar Sykes-Duckworth – Younger son of Henry Sykes-Duckworth, Earl of Malvern. Nephew of Alma and Roger. Student at Oxford. Acolyte of Cyril Lighton.

Gayatri Badarur – Student of medicine at Oxford. Older sister to Sajida.

Sajida Badarur – Fun-loving Princess from Tezpur. Younger sister to Gayatri.

Leslie Dashwood – Close friend to Granville. Thorough rotter.

Julia Aston – Actor and smashing fashion plate. Lover of many people.

Ian Clavering – Theatre producer and also a smashing fashion plate.

Cyril Lighton – Don of politics at Balliol College, Oxford. Mentor to Edgar. An irritating leftist.

Charles Frett – General factotum at Pauncefort Hall. Has a past.

Mabel Lynn – Long-time cook at Pauncefort Hall.

Mary – House- and kitchen-maid at Pauncefort Hall.

Grayling – Cheeky tuxedo cat who rules the roost at Pauncefort Hall.

1

The gingerbread snapped between her fingers. She dunked the half biscuit in her tea and rescued it before it dissolved in the taupe liquid.

Fina Aubrey-Havelock wiped away the steam spreading across the window. She peered out into the inky winter dark. A few windows still glowed with pinpricks of candlelight from across the quad. Tentative snowflakes fell against the pane before being spun into oblivion by a small puff of wind.

She sighed, glancing at the clock on the mantel. Three am. Six hours left to finish this ghastly paper. She smiled to herself, knowing that a completed treatise on a little-known, frightful colonial general meant the start of the winter holiday. Not that there would be much time for luxuriating in the delicious lassitude made so precious by the impending return of the next term. But the holiday would be thrilling nonetheless. She was quite sure of that.

Drawn away from her reverie by the crackle of her candle's flame, Fina buckled down to complete her task. Two hours later, she shuffled her stack of papers into a neat square and laid it upon the desk as if it were a sleeping kitten. Crawling under her icy but ample counterpane, she drifted into a luscious sleep, interrupted only by the occasional plopping of snow piles sliding from the overhang of her window.

"Fina, Fina! Wake up, Fina!"

Fina's heavy lids peeled back slowly, squinting at her friend. The light streaming through the curtains enveloped her in a halo.

"Urgh. Ruby. What time is it?"

"Eight o'clock," Ruby answered. "You must move if you want to submit that paper!"

Fina sat up, and then flopped down again with a groan. Ruby giggled, smoothing her own hair as she gazed at Fina's dishevelled mane. "I forgot how much you love the mornings!" she said.

"Where's your masterpiece?" Ruby twirled around the room until she spied the precious cargo on the desk. "I'm dressed, so I will dash across the quad to submit it for you. In the meantime, you should bathe and pack. We need to catch the 11:25 to Great Malvern if we're to arrive at Pauncefort Hall on time."

"What? Pauncefort Hall? I thought we were going to see Julia Aston this afternoon, at her flat in Chelsea. Don't tell me she's changed her mind? I was so looking forward to taking off my scholar's mortarboard and putting on a more fashionable creation, something better suited to a seamstress. Perhaps that lovely little Valois toque with the ostrich feather."

Ruby laughed. "The ink's barely dry on your history paper, and already you're back in the world of haute couture! Anyway, we're still engaged to work on Julia's wardrobe, but circumstances have changed. She telegraphed me yesterday, saying she'd been invited to spend Christmas at the Hall. She motored down last Tuesday – how she keeps warm in that little Morris, I can't imagine – and apparently she's been singing our praises to her host, Lady Charlotte Sykes-Duckworth. Or should I say, her *dear, her very dear friend*, Lady Charlotte Sykes-Duckworth," said Ruby, allowing a note of mockery to enter her voice as she imitated Julia's theatrical delivery. "When Lady Charlotte heard that we would be coming down to designing Julia's frocks for the next season, including the gown for her film premiere in the new year, she was – reading between the lines of the telegram – simply wild with jealousy. Now she wants us to come down to Pauncefort and sort out her wardrobe, too."

"Another client? But how marvellous," said Fina, sitting up, her drowsiness forgotten.

"Yes, and she wants me to design at least two dresses. At this rate, I shall struggle to get through that crystallography course next term; I'll be too busy studying the Paris catalogues."

Fina smiled to herself. In all the time she had known her friend, Ruby had never once struggled with her studies at Oxford. Her chemistry papers seemed to materialise, fully formed and on time, without any visible effort on her part.

"That's not all," added Ruby. She leaned forward confidentially. "When I mentioned Pauncefort to a certain person – you know who I mean – they said that while we're there, we might perhaps be able to carry out an assignment that would help our cause."

"What sort of assignment?"

"Full details will be offered once we're on the train," said Ruby, tugging at Fina's eiderdown. "Come on, lazy bones. Pack a case and meet me at my room at 10:30. Sharp!"

With that, she scooped up the sheaf of papers and glided out of the room. In the ensuing snow-muffled silence, Fina felt the devilish gremlin of lethargy lulling her back to sleep.

Shaking her head, she got up and marched to the bathroom – determined not to be dishevelled when they arrived at Pauncefort Hall. The bracing air and tepid water of the bath revived her, and she sighed in pleasant anticipation of the weekend.

Breakfast beckoned, but the Great Malvern train wouldn't wait. When she returned to her room, she flung open the doors to her small wardrobe. With one deft movement, she emptied it completely. She had a small selection of clothes, but one that was more than satisfactory. Having a dress designer as a best friend, and as an assistant seamstress herself, Fina certainly had clothes that fitted and suited her personality. They were clean, minimal and a perfectly tailored fit.

She selected a warm, cream-coloured silk blouse, with a line of tiny buttons along a mutton sleeve. Next, a charcoal grey fitted A-line skirt, with a forest green jumper that set off her auburn hair. Her favourite azure day dress, cut in a fine wool and a rather dramatic brocade tea gown satisfied her dual need for propriety and drama. A daring navy silk cocktail gown gifted to her by an associate of Schiaparelli in Paris completed her wardrobe. Rounding it off with two pairs of shoes and a rather jaunty burgundy hat, she folded each item carefully, snuggling them in her large case – reminding her of her grandfather who had given it to her on her fifteenth birthday.

Giving a contented sigh, Fina crossed the room to fetch her dressmakers' kit. She inserted her notebook, pen and two of her favourite books, the leather volume of Jamaican poet Una Marson's *Tropic Reveries* and a collection of Irish nationalist Ethna Carbery's poems. Gathering her kit and suitcase, she glanced around her tidy nook and strode out to meet Ruby in her room.

"There you are!" said Ruby, outstretching her arms as if she hadn't seen her friend in years. "Not a minute to lose," she said, breaking into a gentle trot down the hallway.

The station was a brief ten-minute walk from the college. The pavement was icy enough that she had to tread gingerly, which made her feel rather silly – tiptoeing on the balls of her feet like a small prancing dog. Shivering from the cold and excitement, they reached the platform.

Releasing their heavy loads with a thud on a nearby bench, they rubbed their gloved hands together and stamped their feet. Ruby, dressed to perfection – as always, Fina thought – had on her signature dove-grey travelling suit underneath a long camel overcoat. Melted snowflakes dotted her grey fedora, topped with a slash of finely lined peacock blue. It was daring yet somehow entirely subtle. Indeed, that was precisely how she would describe her friend and collaborator.

Once on the train, they ensconced themselves in a corner table for a late breakfast. Fina soon found herself munching happily on a thick slice of toast, slathered with a generous portion of marmalade.

"Mhm, that's delicious," said Ruby, sipping her tea. Then she placed her cup in its saucer as if it were the final piece of a puzzle. She let out a long breath, pursing her lips into an oval.

Fina cocked her head to one side. "Why the sigh?"

Ruby gifted her with a wan smile. "Oh, I'm actually quite pleased. We have two clients, both of whom travel in exalted circles. But I've a feeling that this weekend may prove to be a challenging one for us." Looking as if she had convinced herself that they were up for the challenge, she steeled herself and continued.

"Let's begin with Julia Aston – you saw her last spring at the Gaiety in *My Word, Melinda!*, didn't you? Well, rumour has it that she's not the easiest leading lady to work with. I believe half the reason she's asked us to look over her wardrobe is because she doesn't entirely trust the costume designers on this new film. It's her first, and she has her eye on Hollywood, you know. Luckily for us, the picture is set in the modern era, so we won't have to bother with a costume drama."

"Have you met her?"

"I was introduced to her once at a party for one of her shows. She is somewhat abrupt and yet..." Ruby halted, looking at her teacup in distaste.

"Is there something wrong with the tea?" asked Fina.

Ruby shook her head. "It's strange, that. People as blunt as she is usually rub me up the wrong way."

Fina said, "You seem to like me and I'm rather blunt."

"Aha! You have me there, dearest one. But you do it for all the right reasons. And you can wax lyrical when you want to, I've noticed," said Ruby, emitting her hallmark giggle with little hiccoughs in between. "In any case," she added, "it seems to add to her charm. She shouldn't be too dreadful to work for if her existing wardrobe is anything to go by – positively edgy – exactly our cup of tea," said Ruby, raising her cup in a salute to Fina. She nibbled on her piece of toast and gave a contented look out the window.

"Yes," said Fina, "I believe I saw her photograph in *Tatler* last month, and she was wearing the most divine day dress. But I don't believe I know her bosom-friend – what did you say her name was?"

"Charlotte Sykes-Duckworth," murmured Ruby. "Did you never hear of her from Edgar Sykes-Duckworth? He's at Balliol, so you may have bumped into him on your way to the Sheldonian."

"My dear, we hardly mix in the same circles! I suppose he's her brother? I never saw him with any other member of his family. He always seemed to be very wrapped up in his studies, and his work with the Labour Club."

"Well, he and Lady Charlotte, plus their older brother Granville, are all installed currently in the ancestral lair, Pauncefort. Charlotte is every inch the *lady*." Ruby said, with an exaggerated wagging of her little finger while sipping the remainder of her tea.

"Evesham, fifteen minutes," boomed the ticket collector as he rumbled past their table.

Pouring the last of the tea, Fina asked in hushed tones, "Could you tell me about our mysterious assignment?"

Glancing around, then leaning in to speak in her characteristically confident manner, Ruby said, "Yes. It has to do with their business in the colonies. The Sykes-Duckworths, you know, made their fortune in sugar: the head of the family, Lord Malvern, owns some plantations in St Kitts. He is ruthless, to the point of brutality. Last year, some of the workers staged a rebellion, and the Sykes-Duckworths enlisted the support of the local constabulary to quell the resistance. But it didn't all go to plan. There were fatalities, and the plantation owners were the ones responsible. Remember my cousin I told you about, who died last year? He was caught up in it; I didn't tell you at the time, but he was one of the casualties."

"Oh, Ruby – I'm so sorry."

Ruby took a breath and carried on. "Granville Sykes-Duckworth, the eldest son, was there with his father at the time, and he most likely played a central role – he may even have been the one to direct the violence."

"But there's not much we can do to undermine him if there's no proof."

Ruby's eyes sparkled. "Ah, but there is! One police sergeant was so appalled by the sugar barons' cruelty that he wrote an eyewitness account of the whole affair. He put it all on paper due to a heavy conscience and to protect himself against possible retribution by the plantation owners. The papers fell into the hands of the family, however. We know they brought them back to Pauncefort, though we don't know what they plan to do with them. If the papers are published, the scandal might bring down not only Lord Malvern and Granville, but the entire sugar empire of their company, Lavington's. It has a chokehold on the island. I suspect we'll find out more once we get our hands on those papers."

"They'll certainly make interesting reading over the toast and marmalade. And who do we give them to once we've got them?"

"I've not got a name just yet. As usual, my brother Wendell didn't tell me about anyone else who is involved in our cause – for our own protection. It's entirely possible that someone at Pauncefort is our contact. I won't know until they give me a signal. It's also possible that they are not at Pauncefort, in which case I'll find them when we return to Oxford."

"Well, I shall try to contain my curiosity. But one more question: where do we find these papers?"

"I haven't a clue," Ruby said, her eyes puckering to mirror her impish grin.

2

On the platform, Fina and Ruby gripped their hats against the fierce wind as they scurried into the station. A man in a cool forest green uniform strode up to meet them, confidently, Fina noted, as they were the only ones inside the station. Though the buttons on his uniform stood stiffly at attention, she could not help but notice the rather raffish tilt of his cap.

Scooping up their suitcases, he said, "You must be Miss Dove and Miss Aubrey-Havelock. I'm Charles Frett, your driver to Pauncefort Hall." Ruby gave Fina her quick, but unmistakable wink.

Murmuring agreement and relief, they hurried into the Rolls-Royce outside the station, escaping the chill from the strong wind. Fina sighed as if she were slipping into a steaming hot bath as she nestled into the soft black cushion of her seat.

"Is there much more snow predicted for the weekend?"

"A great deal, I'm afraid, miss," said Charles. "I'm not sure how it will affect the guests arriving later this afternoon and evening. I hope I shall be able to drive them to Pauncefort. We have quite the guest list this weekend."

"Oh?" Ruby said, with the air of an ingénue. "I thought it was only the family – as well as Julia Aston. Who are the others?"

Charles let out a whoosh of air, as if he were unburdening himself from a great weight. "Well, miss, as Master Granville will be graduating Oxford early, in anticipation of his move to join his father in the Caribbean, he decided to plan this weekend as a graduation-cum-Christmas celebration of sorts." Charles placed an emphasis on the word Oxford – an emphasis that indicated great derision.

Deciding to file away this information for later, Fina continued, "So, these guests are affiliated with Oxford? We just finished the term. I submitted my final paper – or I should say, Ruby submitted my final paper this morning," she said, patting the shoulder of her friend.

Through the rear-view mirror, Fina saw the stricken look on Charles' face as he realised his blunder.

"Oh, do forgive me, miss. I didn't mean anything by it."

Ruby plunged forward, seemingly sensing his embarrassment.

"I'm simply *dying* to know if we're acquainted with any of these other guests because of the Oxford connection."

"Right, miss," said Charles, releasing his clenched jaw. "There's Cyril Lighton, a don at Oxford. I'm not sure of his area of study. I do know there are rumours he is a radical of some sort."

Fina noticed that he said the word 'radical' without the usual derision reserved for that term, and decided that she liked this Charles.

He continued. "Then there's Leslie Dashwood, a friend of Granville's from Oxford. Mr Dashwood works with the Brownshirts."

A fascist! Ruby and Fina exchanged a wary glance as they

crested the hill. The car sputtered a bit – though in a manner befitting a Rolls – choking at the incline.

Crunch. Fina fell against Ruby as they came to a halt.

"So sorry. I'll scrape the window to remove the ice and snow before we continue down this hill," he said, slamming the door as he stepped out.

Pushing her hat back into place, Ruby whispered, "This Charles is a peculiar sort of driver. He seems a cut above, judging by the way he speaks."

"I had the same thought myself!" responded Fina. "Did you see his reaction when we mentioned Oxford?"

Click. The car door opened to reveal a ruddy-faced Charles. "I apologize for the delay, ladies. Not long now."

At the bottom of what must be a lush green valley in the summer, she saw an imposing, but strangely compact Elizabethan manor house. Fina thought Pauncefort looked rather like a gift box, without the ribbon to offer colour. The snow blanketed the grounds, with drifts already kissing the bottom windowpanes as a result of the freshening wind.

As the Rolls came to a halt in front of the grey stone facade, an impressively coifed older man approached them with a glide that defied the presence of ice on the drive.

"Grimston, our faithful butler," Charles said with notable fondness.

Grimston offered to help the women out of the car and into the warmth, while Charles unloaded their luggage. Skidding on the ice, Ruby entered the hall a few steps behind Fina.

"Miss Dove, how splendid to meet you at last!" said a cascading, beautiful voice. Fina looked up from her feet to see a weeping-willow of a woman – tall, rail thin, but not frail. Her cobalt brocade dress with a high collar framed her triangular face and gave her an added air of formality. Fina judged her understated but exquisitely fashionable. The one defiant touch was her long, dark hair, swept up in an inexplicably rakish yet pleasing chignon. Her green eyes held no hint of her personality, though her primly pursed lips clashed with the warmth of her voice. "I'm Charlotte Sykes-Duckworth. Welcome to Pauncefort."

"Oh, Lady Charlotte, I'm afraid you're mistaken. I'm Fina Aubrey-Havelock, a friend and assistant to Ruby Dove," replied Fina, as the familiar warmth crept up her neck and into her cheeks like ivy growing around a tree.

Ruby stepped forward and held out her gloved hand to Charlotte. "So pleased to meet you, Lady Charlotte."

Jolted out of her composure, Charlotte rapidly opened her lips and closed them again, like a hungry goldfish. Her eyes widened momentarily.

Not missing a beat, Ruby said, "I expect you may have never met someone whose mother is a real native of St Kitts." She said it calmly, without challenge, though the statement clearly needed no emotion to bolster it.

Fina was quite accustomed to Lady Charlotte's mistake, followed by the reaction to her friend's appearance. A twinge of guilt flitted through her stomach at her inward pleasure at the discomfort Ruby caused among the aristocracy.

"I, ah, well... My family, you see..." Charlotte faltered, then recovered. "Yes, of course I have. As you must know, my family has business interests in the Caribbean." She continued, as if nothing had happened, and said, "So pleased to meet you at last. I cannot wait to see what you have in store for my wardrobe! And please do call me Charlotte." Her mask of formality had been lowered again, beginning with her half-closed eyelids. What was hidden behind those eyelids? Was this just a typical aristocratic distance? No, surely not, thought Fina. There was something definitely incongruous about Lady Charlotte's facade.

Lowering her hunched shoulders, Charlotte continued on

with a momentum that Fina thought must surely be a mark of her personality. "Now, you must be tired from your journey. I'll have Grimston show you to your rooms on the second floor. You can unpack, and then ring the bell and the maid will show you to my room. I'd like for you to see my wardrobe first so we can match it with the latest fashions. Are you peckish?"

"Thank you – we had a delicious meal on the train," replied Ruby.

Ruby and Fina followed Grimston's rapid, yet precise steps to the second floor. Pauncefort Hall, despite its somewhat bleak exterior, had a cheery warmth about it, appropriate to Christmastime. Fina felt her mood shift as she inhaled the air, redolent with nutmeg.

As they rounded the first staircase, Fina asked, "Grimston, the decorations are delightful. Do you do this every year?"

"Yes, miss. The Earl insists on full Yuletide decorations every year," he said, pointing at the sprigs of mistletoe in each doorway they passed. "The Countess directs the decoration, of course..." He trailed off, apparently assuming this was self-explanatory.

Fina shot an enquiring look at Ruby. "Didn't you say he was in St Kitts?" she murmured, slowing down so that Grimston would move out of hearing range.

"That's Charlotte's father, Henry," Ruby whispered. "He only comes back once a year or so. The Countess is his younger sister, and she and the Earl manage the household while Henry – Lord Malvern – is abroad."

It's all very well for some, thought Fina as she took in the darkly gleaming panelling of the wide hallway and the soft hues of the Persian rugs that lined the floor. A sudden shaft of light made them leap into full colour as Grimston opened the door to Fina's bedroom.

"Eee... it's lovely!" she squeaked. Grimston's face remained impassive, though Fina swore she saw a flicker of his eyelids. "This is the most beautiful room I will have ever slept in," she said, halting with embarrassment about her remarks revealing her background. Though her double-barrelled surname signalled status and wealth, Fina's only inheritance was debt. She was as poor as one of those proverbial church mice. Her mind wandered back to Donegal, picturing her grandmother hunched over her favourite books. She said a prayer of thanks to her for helping her get to Oxford.

A fire crackled in the fireplace which was adorned with juniper trimmings. On the mantel, she saw a row of robin-egg blue miniature teacups. The room was painted an unusual rich mahogany colour with sage green accents. The large, plush four-poster bed in the middle of the room looked inviting, especially after the many weeks spent on the unforgiving mattress at college. Resisting the urge to flounce onto the bed, she turned to thank Grimston. He had already floated out of the room.

Sitting on the edge of the bed with a sigh, she heard a light tap at the adjoining door. Before she could rise to open it, Ruby tiptoed in. A velvet bag Fina knew to be her design kit, slung casually over her shoulder, indicated she was ready to depart for Charlotte's room.

"Isn't this a sumptuous room? I wouldn't call the Queen my aunt," said Fina in a whisper, her eyes large and shining. Ruby smiled. "Yes, it is. My room is lovely as well. But what do you mean about the Queen?"

"Ah, it's just an Irish saying. It means that nothing could improve the situation."

"I wish we weren't here to work so we could really enjoy it. But we haven't much time before we go to Charlotte's consultation," Ruby said in a hushed tone that mimicked Fina's.

"Why are we whispering?"

"Good point. I suppose it's good practise for what we're about to do," replied Ruby.

She removed her bag and rummaged around inside it until she found a box of cards, decorated in an ornate pattern with a rather impulsive-looking King on one side and an impudent Jack on the other. Fina looked at her quizzically. Signalling to Fina to put out her hands, Ruby opened the flap and turned it over, dropping the deck into her cupped hands.

Fina cradled the cards as if they were the Holy Grail, waiting for the next set of instructions. Ruby plucked the deck from her hands and fanned them out toward her friend. Fina spied a folded piece of paper among the blue and white patterned cards.

Unfolding the accordion-like paper revealed a floor plan of Pauncefort Hall. Fuzzy blood-red dots adorned some of the rooms.

"I assume the dots represent the rooms where the papers are likely to be found," said Fina, feeling proud of herself for her mental acuity, especially given her lack of sleep.

Ruby nodded. "A friend of mine who knows one of the maids here made out the map – under false pretences, of course. After we begin the initial consultation with Charlotte, I'll say that I don't need you to stay and that you can take a nap if you'd like."

"What should I say after that?"

"Then you'll refuse and say that you'd like to wander around a bit. That's when you can start to make your way through the rooms. Begin with the bedrooms that are marked because we won't be able to access them after guests arrive. We'll have to search the study and other rooms downstairs this evening – after everyone is asleep."

Gently murmuring her assent, Fina asked, "What are we looking for, exactly?"

"I'm not certain what form the papers will take – if they'll be located in an obvious place or locked away in a safe – but I can tell you about the general contents. As I mentioned, the papers concern Granville Sykes-Duckworth's involvement in the sugar company and the St Kitts rebellion. The rebellion happened in Bluegate in March of 1933, and the company's name is Lavington's. There is also a London office, so keep that in mind when looking for addresses."

Fina cocked her head to one side. "Why wouldn't Granville simply burn the papers? Why keep something so damaging to him and the company?"

Ruby's hands clenched. "Because it's his insurance. I'm sure others would like to get their hands on them – let's call them the Bluegate papers. If they were released, the scandal would bring down Lavington's entire sugar empire, not only in St Kitts, but also in other places in the Caribbean. All the other sugar importers would love to see Lavington's fall so they could claw back some of the market."

"But why would Granville keep the Bluegate papers if they're so incriminating?"

"Oh, he wasn't the only one. He knows that if their truth is accepted, these papers will also bring down half the senior staff of the company, not to mention the various authority figures who have turned a blind eye. Those papers are his safety net. As long as he has them, the company is forced to promote him and no one can be held responsible for all of the deaths at the hands of this horrid company."

"I see," said Fina. "So other guests may have dual purposes this weekend? Maybe they represent industrial competitors? Or have other interests?"

"Perhaps," said Ruby. "We'll have to be patient – it takes time to find an ant's belly."

3

Inside Charlotte's cavernous dressing room, Ruby and Fina stared at a bewildering array of gowns. They were strewn in heaps like islands of colour against the calm blue walls. Fina's eyes widened in disbelief.

"I apologize for the state of my room," said Charlotte, clenching her jaw. "I just wasn't sure where to begin, so I thought I'd pull out everything so you could see what I had already."

Fina saw Ruby's shoulders relax. Clearly, Charlotte expected her to take charge. Remembering a particularly nasty incident in Paris, involving a snooty, one-foot-in-the-grave Duchess and her ever-widening waistline and wardrobe, Fina was grateful for Charlotte's attitude. She supposed it was to be expected that their clients were demanding, but really, had it been necessary to demand that Ruby recite the material used in every Chanel frock from the previous season?

"You have so many beautiful pieces," Ruby said, skimming her fingers over a peach silk evening gown. "But I think we should start from scratch and envision what you want your finished wardrobe to look like. Then we may return to what you already have and keep what fits."

"Splendid!" said Charlotte, sighing with relief. "Let's sit down here," she said, pointing to a Victorian set of high-backed chairs in the corner.

As Charlotte perched erect on the edge of the chair, Fina thought she looked as if someone were pushing her off the seat. Her hands sat in a tight ball in her lap. Was she nervous about her clothes or something else entirely? Wasn't a wardrobe fitting supposed to be a delight rather than a trial?

Peering out the window at the light snowfall – normally a pleasant sight – only raised Fina's own anxiety about her mission. Seizing on a moment of silence she said, "I know I am more helpful once we get to the actual design and sewing stage for individual pieces. Why don't I leave you two alone to talk?"

Ruby pulled out her favourite sketchbook, signalling approval of Fina's suggestion. Fina continued, "I would love to take a peek around Pauncefort. The design and colours are sublime. Would you object to me poking about a bit?"

"Of course, Miss Aubrey-Hav – I mean, Fina. Please do. Guests will arrive soon, but I imagine you'll just miss them before they settle into their rooms. Cocktails will be served at six in the drawing room."

As she closed the door gently behind her, she heard Ruby say, "You'll love this evening cape with an emerald lining..."

Though Fina knew she wasn't as clever as her slightly older friend – by one year – she did possess a picture-perfect memory. She relied on it now to recall the map details: red blots of ink splashed merrily across the page, as if a mischievous child had begun an ill-fated art project. She decided to begin with Granville's room. Grateful for the ample spread of thick rugs in the corridor, she crept toward an elaborate, carved door at the end of the passage. After giving it a tentative tap, she slipped into the spacious room.

Contrary to her mental image of Granville as an unkempt cad, the room was spotless. The furniture and meagre knick-knacks were set out with military precision. The armchairs, despite their soft innards, stood to attention in a permanent salute. Granville's essential personality was confirmed, however, by the noticeable lack of books.

At least it would be easy to search if she didn't have to inter-rogate books by shaking them violently, she thought. The only paper item in the room was a small pamphlet by Oswald Mosley on the nightstand. Making her way through the room in a methodical fashion, she opened drawers, sliding her fingers underneath, hoping for concealed papers and riffled through his wardrobe. She even felt around the inside edges of the unlit fire-place – recalling that technique from a favourite detective story.

"Ah-choo!" she sneezed in the dust. Ear cocked, she listened for movement in the hallway. Sensing nothing, she crept into the adjoining bathroom. This was also immaculate, furnished only with a creamy coloured claw-foot bath in the corner and a cabinet above the washbasin. Opening it, she saw Granville's compulsive order complex carried into his personal hygiene practices. An emerald bottle of aftershave, a small brown bottle labelled 'brain salt', a new toothbrush, a straight-edge razor and strop, a bar of soap and a small, half-full tin of Calox tooth powder – all squared off at attention. She felt disappointed by her lack of progress as she left the bathroom by the other door, which opened into the corridor.

Congratulating herself on the efficiency of her search, she leaned on the balcony to contemplate her next move. She peered over the square spiral staircase to the ground-floor hallway.

She sniffed. Cigar smoke?

"Enjoying the view?"

Fina spun round to confront a tall man, leering at her with ice-grey eyes. The words wafting out of his mouth were less noticeable than the mixed odour of Scotch and cigar escaping the same orifice. With a deft move away from his inappropriate physical proximity, Fina inched backward. Pursing her lips, she said, "I'm Fina Aubrey-Havelock. I don't believe we've met."

"Well we have now," he responded with a wink. He slicked back his already-receding hairline, as if any strand could possibly escape the plaster he used as hair pomade.

"Sir, I really don't think..."

"Now, now. It's all just a bit of fun. I'm Leslie Dashwood. Best chum of Granville's down at Oxford," he said, seeming to regain a bit of composure as he uttered his clipped sentences. The effect was cancelled by a wanton swig at his heavy cut-glass tumbler. Fina thought he looked as tranquil and pleased as a basking shark.

"I thought guests weren't arriving yet. I was just having a look around," said Fina, continuing to inch away.

Swinging his glass to make his point, nearly spraying Fina with a miniature tidal wave of Scotch, Leslie continued. "Yes, well, I motored down last night to Great Malvern to stay at a local inn."

Not feeling compelled to explain, he changed the subject. "Aubrey-Havelock... Aubrey-Havelock. That name rings a bell."

"Yes, my father was part of the Tavistock Aubrey-Havelock line. Perhaps you've been to Tavistock?" Fina said, lightly, hoping that the alcohol would impair his memory from following this line of enquiry any further.

"Yes, but that's not it... I've got it!" he said, holding up an index finger in triumph. "Are you related to Connor Aubrey-Havelock? That chap hanged for murdering his father?" Fina saw a slight smirk emerge from the corner of his thin-lipped mouth.

Fina dug her fingernails into her arm.

"Yes... I remember the headlines," he continued, waving his drink so excitedly that Fina hoped he would be deprived of further liquid pleasure. "Irish son murders father, Earl of Tavistock, in a fit of rage." Not remembering his audience, or not caring if he did, he motored on, "Yes, even though he had English noble blood in his veins, it couldn't cancel out the savage Irish blood."

By this time, Fina felt her face had become as crimson as the rug on the floor. Wobbling on her legs, she turned and dashed down the corridor before the tears tumbled forth.

Fleeing her tormenter, Fina stopped to catch her breath – but more importantly to wipe away her tears in front of a gilt-edged mirror in a small recess off the main hall. As she looked at her splotchy, freckled face, another round of tears welled up, from what felt like her toes. She removed her handkerchief – eternally grateful for the ingenious pockets Ruby had designed in her dress – and dabbed her eyes. Would the pain ever go away? Or at least be dulled by that maddening cliché of time? Connor... Her jaw tightened with the now-familiar transition from sadness to rage. A rage that fuelled her. Gave her purpose. Tucking her unruly, wavy hair behind one ear, she sniffed and plastered a smile on her face that belied the torment underneath. She must focus on the task at hand.

Tap-tap. After knocking on the nearest door and hearing nothing, Fina escaped inside. She did not know if this room was on her ink-blot map. Through bleary eyes, she struggled to find her bearings. A rapid scan of the lived-in room revealed it was one of the family bedrooms rather than guest quarters. Though the room was hardly disorderly, it somehow felt more human than Granville's room. Perhaps it was the fact that the stack of books on the nightstand, for example, were slightly askew. No political literature for this member of the family. The faded gold titles on the spines read *Othello* and *Beowulf*. Hmph, thought Fina. Serious reading. Her eyes crinkled with delight when she read the spine on the top: Wilkie Collins' *Moonstone*.

Moving on, her eyes fixed on a small mahogany roll-top writing desk in the corner of the room. Rubbing her hands together and blowing into them, as much from the chill as from her encounter with Leslie Dashwood, she marched over to the desk. The surface held one small framed photograph of a woman with a child, aged three or four, perched on her knee. By the style of the woman's dress, Fina judged the photo to be least fifteen years old. The mother's thick mane cascaded about her shoulders, half hiding a contented smile. The little boy's legs looked as if they had just been swinging about the mother's knee, complementing the joyful grin on his face. Recalling fond memories of her own mother, she fought back the grief welling up from her already exhausted tear ducts. Shaking her head, she said aloud, "Fina!" just like her mother had said when she was in trouble as a child. Rolling back the top of the desk revealed writing paper, pens, envelopes and a few closed drawers.

The tiny drawers divulged little of interest. Fina flicked through the carelessly assembled papers: race meeting schedules, college reading lists, tobacconists' bills, and lists of figures which meant nothing to her. One sheaf of paper was particularly thick and incomprehensible. 'Due Diligence Report: Dulcet & Sons' was the heading, followed by: 'Based on Files Examined, With Particular Regards to Foreign & Colonial Assets, Property and Debentures'. Fina frowned. If only it had been seventeenth-century English, or basic Latin, she might have stood a chance of understanding it. As for the columns of numbers running down the sheet, they must be sums of money

– at least, the ones marked with £ must be – but what about the others?

She turned the page and her eye was immediately caught by a handwritten scribble across the top: 'NOW'. It was underlined twice, and the writing was emphatic enough that the pen nib had nearly torn through the paper. Whoever wrote that had been desperate, she thought. Desperate for some action to be taken straight away. But what? How could this dry financial statement inspire such panicked urgency in whoever had held the pen?

She straightened up, carefully restoring the items to their homes, and eased the top of the desk back into place. Now on to the wardrobe. Opening it revealed a row of tweed blazers, pressed trousers, a few jumpers and a row of brown shoes of varying styles. All expensively tailored, of course, but not particularly avant-garde in the men's department.

Satisfied, she made her exit with a rapid, efficient step, ready to report her findings to Ruby.

Fina tended to worry. This, she knew, was one of her signature accomplishments in life. Though she was only twenty-one years old, she had learned through bitter experience that sometimes, one's worst fears really did come true. But she had survived and even thrived. Ruby, while also introspective – and someone who had already survived tragedies in her life – did not tend to worry, or at least not as much as Fina did. Early-life calamities had shaped their personalities in quite contrasting, yet oddly complementary ways. Both were loyal to a few people, and mistrust ruled much of their actions. Ruby turned this outward – she trusted almost no one but herself. Fina, however, turned it inward – she mistrusted herself. This was one of the reasons she was drawn to Ruby. Despite her other faults, Ruby trusted herself.

"Ruby, I'm anxious. Do you think we'll get caught?"

"Of course not, Feens. And that gown is divine. You look positively delicious in it," Ruby proclaimed. Admiring her curved reflection in the mirror, Fina smiled. She had to immodestly agree with her friend – just this once.

"You're not too shabby yourself," she told Ruby. By custom

and by trade, Ruby looked stunning in her figure-skimming blue tulle satin dress. Subtle sequins sparkled along the vertical lines of the dress. Her hair was perfectly coifed, of course, and she wore her pinprick opal earrings that made her skin glow.

"Charlotte has definite ideas about what she wants, but I am thrilled she has ordered so many new pieces." Arranging herself on the overstuffed settee, Ruby said, "But let's talk about the important news. Tell me – I'm dying to know what you've found out so far."

Fina recounted her adventures faithfully, omitting the hurtful words of Leslie Dashwood. She didn't want to be consoled. At least not yet.

"Hmm... I wish I'd seen those financial papers," said Ruby. "Are you sure they weren't about Lavington's?"

"Positively. The name on it was quite different, and I didn't see anything about sugar."

"I'd think they weren't important," mused Ruby, "if it weren't for that note written so urgently across the top. Someone may be planning drastic action – perhaps even this weekend. I don't like the look of it, frankly. Perhaps we'll know more once we find the Bluegate papers." She rose and went to the dressing table, where she opened a tiny pot of eyelash-black and began to apply it carefully. "What about the photograph – do you think you'd recognize the child in it as an adult?"

"Perhaps. I'm not sure if the child is one of the current family – such as Edgar, Granville's brother – or if he's some other member of the family. In any case, we can confirm it is Edgar's room by the type of clothes he wears tonight."

"Why? Are they as divine as your dress?" giggled Ruby.

"Hardly. Rather drab and boring – though expensive, of course. Speaking of the opposite of boring, what is our plan for tonight?"

"We'll have to search the study tonight, perhaps quite late.

Let's gather as much information from all the guests as possible. We should suss out their connections to the Sykes-Duckworths as well as the Earl and Countess of Snittlegarth. Wendell is expecting a full report, as well as finding the Bluegate papers. I'm counting on your photographic memory to come through for us."

"I hope it will." Fina paced in front of the fireplace. "I'm nervous."

"Yes, I am too. A couple of cocktails – though not too many – should do the trick. Try to enjoy yourself!" With that, the drinks gong sounded from below. Ruby signalled to Fina that they should strut their way downstairs.

Giving one another a quick squeeze of the hand, Ruby and Fina slinked into the din of the drawing room.

"There you are!" Charlotte purred as they entered, lifting her glass in salute. She was resplendent in an emerald green silk Schiaparelli with a long V-neck in the back – quite a daring departure from her signature style. Despite Charlotte's warm welcome, Fina winced at the grip of her hand on her upper arm as she piloted the two friends around the room for introductions.

The drawing room, like all of the rooms Fina had seen at Pauncefort Hall thus far, was decorated meticulously from top to bottom. It was aglow with candles, placed far away from the luscious green trimmings of holly and juniper boughs. Clearly, not far enough, thought Fina. She spied a glass set precariously close to one of the candles. The candle tipped and caused a minor conflagration. Charlotte rushed to douse the flame with her glass of water.

Gliding back toward them – deftly avoiding her already slightly swaying guests – Charlotte resumed her mission.

"Uncle Roger insists on these dreadful lighted candles everywhere at Christmastime. Such a hazard," she said, smiling and shaking her head as if he were a cute but bothersome child.

Taking a quick glance at her silver watch, she said under her breath, "We're running a bit behind schedule. Would you mind terribly if I pointed people out to you? Then you'll know who everyone is in case we get interrupted in the middle of in-person introductions."

"Of course," said Fina readily, wincing as she remembered her earlier 'in-person' introduction to Leslie Dashwood.

"Splendid," said Charlotte. "Let's start in the corner, with the Oxford contingent. That rather sulky young man with the sandy hair, drab colours and slightly too-tight collar is my brother, Edgar. You may have seen him before – he's at Balliol. That man he's speaking to, with the high forehead, glasses, moustache and rather sharp suit by Frederick Scholte, is Cyril Lighton, a don at his college. I suspect you may know of him already."

Grimston appeared from the ether to speak to Charlotte in a whisper.

Fina used this momentary diversion to eye the don. Cyril Lighton clasped his hands tightly behind his back, bobbing and weaving slightly as a response to his companion's conversation. His tooth-combed moustache gleamed in a startling fashion, drawing attention away from an almost-absent chin. Having had many recent experiences watching dons closely during a lecture of one sort or another, this one ran to type. And yet. There was something that set him apart.

She felt a nudge at her shoulder. Without speaking, Ruby motioned with her eyes toward the floor. Fina looked down. That was it. Cyril was leaning against a bookcase, causing his trouser legs to ride up a little. Peeking out rather cheekily from under the trouser legs was one white sock and one red sock. *Quelle horreur!* She snorted a bit, trying to suppress a giggle.

Ruby held a hand up to her scarlet lips, only letting out what sounded like a hiccough.

As Charlotte was still engaged, Fina turned to consider Edgar. The clothes confirmed that the room she had searched earlier had belonged to him and she thought it possible that he was the child in the photograph. She would know if he grinned, but that seemed like an unlikely possibility at this point.

Near his feet, flecks of white, mirroring the snow outside, drifted to the floor. Fina attributed this to Edgar's habit of picking at the skin around his thumbs. His fingers moved with an urgent, incessant grating behaviour, as if he had been stung by a nettle.

Half fascinated, half disgusted by Edgar's proclivities, Fina pulled her attention back to Charlotte who had turned away from the ethereal Grimston and drifted toward the fireplace, clearly expecting her to follow. "Come, you simply must meet Uncle Roger. He minds the shop here at Pauncefort while my father is engaged on business in the Caribbean, as he generally is nine months out of the twelve. Don't be fooled by that rather old-fashioned monocle; it makes Uncle Roger look rather a stuffed shirt, but he's a darling really." That last was spoken in a whisper as the Earl of Snittlegarth turned to greet them.

"Enchanted, Miss Aubrey-Havelock," he boomed, taking Fina's hand and executing a courtly half-bow over it. "It's an uncommon pleasure to have so many fresh faces here at Pauncefort for Christmas. Yes, yes, quite uncommon." His eyes crinkled up almost to the point of disappearing as he beamed at Fina.

Here was a man who clearly enjoyed his wine and his food. The Earl's pink complexion was heightened by reddish broken capillaries along his bulbous nose and the buttons strained to be free from the tyranny of his waistcoat. His rather unfashionable grey mutton chops added definition to his jowls. Fina instinctively recoiled from his touch, repelled by the weight of all the

Earl represented, his centuries-old heritage of privilege and dominion – and yet, she found him to be a quite likable looking character. "So kind of you to have us down," she murmured.

"Miss Dove, a joy, an absolute joy, to welcome you to Pauncefort," the Earl carried on, giving Ruby the same treatment he'd given Fina. "And Charlotte tells me the two of you are some of London's finest... er... frock-makers, is it?"

"Dress designers, sir," replied Ruby firmly.

The word must have caught the ear of the woman the Earl had been talking to, because at that point she turned and gracefully inserted herself into the conversation, tilting her head curiously at Ruby and Fina.

"Sajida Badarur," announced Charlotte, "a princess from Tezpur. She is visiting her sister, Gayatri, whom you can just about see over there by the rather garish mirror, in the taupe crêpe de Chine."

It was hardly surprising that any mention of dress had attracted the princess' attention, thought Fina. Sajida's Chanel gown was the very height of elegance; it must have come from last season's collection, and it fitted her slim form perfectly.

"A pleasure," murmured Sajida.

"Gayatri is reading medicine at Somerville College, Oxford," Charlotte went on, "and I believe that when Edgar heard that she and her sister had never experienced a traditional English Christmas, he felt he simply had to invite them to share ours."

"Dashed shame to miss the Yuletide, hey?" said the Earl. "Jolliest time of the year – bar the Glorious Twelfth, that is, ho ho!"

Ruby chucked dutifully, but her eyes narrowed as they met Fina's. Charlotte, conscious that a chill had descended, took their arms and hastened them away.

"Oh dear, I was so focused on introductions that I failed to be a good host! Where is your liquid tonic?" said Charlotte, looking in Grimston's direction. Grimston materialized with a tray of champagne and luridly colourful cocktails. Fina selected a glass of champagne, her favourite, but also a drink whose effects could be measured more easily than a cocktail. Ruby, somewhat out of character – though she could afford it since she could hold her liquor better than Fina – selected what appeared to be a martini from the drinks tray.

Now that Charlotte's champagne had been topped up, she continued on her merry round of introductions. "We're nearly there! The man in the opposite corner by the window – my, the snow is coming down – sorry, the man with the close-cropped hair, striped cravat and impeccable shoes, is Ian Clavering, the theatre producer, you know. He lives half the year in London during theatre season and then goes home for the other half to the Bahamas to be with family. Have you seen any of his shows? Of course, I don't suppose you get down to the West End much, from Oxford," said Charlotte vaguely.

"Not as much as I'd like," admitted Ruby. "I've seen Mr Clavering here and there, but I don't believe we've been introduced."

Taking the hint, Charlotte began leading them to the window-seat, then drew up short and stopped. Ian Clavering's lanky figure was leaning closely in toward a woman with a brown helmet-like bob and close-set eyes. Fina's stomach flipped with jealousy at the height of her cheekbones. They were deep in conversation, oblivious to the laughter and chat of the other guests. Ian's eyebrows wriggled with what appeared to be disbelief – either that or intense consternation. His square jaw worked itself in a haphazard motion, slipping occasionally as his eyebrows lifted.

"Perhaps the introduction can wait," said Ruby, sensing Charlotte's reluctance to interrupt the pair. "He and Julia must be dishing the dirt on some scandal at the Criterion."

With an air of relief, Charlotte said, "Of course, you know my dear friend Julia, don't you – you're arranging her wardrobe for this new film. Some sort of... thriller, I believe." She said the word as if it were the name of a disease. Fina doubted Charlotte had ever seen a film in her life. For herself, though, it was quite exciting to see Julia Aston – *the* Julia Aston – only several feet away. "Her red suit from Gilbert Adrian is marvellous, isn't it?" said Charlotte, back on safe ground. "I must say I am pleased with the sartorial quality of our guests this weekend," she added with a satisfied sigh.

"And lastly, we come to more of the Sykes-Duckworth brood," Charlotte said, gesticulating with her glass toward the entrance to the room. A drop or two of the champagne escaped onto the floor. Fina was glad it was almost time for dinner. She hadn't eaten since lunch and felt that the champagne was already going to her head – as it was apparently for Charlotte and the rest of the guests if the volume level of discussion in the drawing room were any indication.

"The rather pleasant looking woman in the rose-coloured frock – it suits her even though it is a bit out of fashion – is my dear auntie, the Countess of Snittlegarth." Lady Snittlegarth's voluminous sleeves rippled as she flapped her arms with abandon. She must be in the midst of an excellent story. Fina warmed to this aunt, with her crown of slate grey hair, coiled like a somewhat amateur Chelsea bun atop her oval-shaped head.

"I love both my aunt and uncle dearly," Charlotte added in a confidential tone. Fina smiled, but wondered why she felt the need to make the declaration.

At that moment, the Earl of Snittlegarth, making a dramatic point with his hands by the fireplace, dislodged one of the candles from the mantelpiece. In what seemed like slow motion, Fina watched as the candle wobbled like a hard-boiled egg and then catapulted off the edge of the mantelpiece into oblivion. With surprisingly quick reflexes, the Earl caught the candle, but not before it splattered tallow on Gayatri's cocoa-coloured dress. "Oh my dear, I am so dreadfully sorry," he said with a quavering voice.

"Please do not trouble yourself," replied Gayatri, whose words belied the look of frustration in her eyes. She peeled the wax off the crêpe, leaving a splotch behind. Her sister bent down to examine it more closely, nearly providing comic relief by bumping heads with Ruby, who had deftly sidled up to the Earl as soon as the candle had tumbled.

Ruby held out her hand to introduce herself to Gayatri, then Sajida, followed by the Earl. By this time, a crowd had gathered around the fireplace to see the drama unfold.

Ruby bent down and said, looking at the spot on the dress, "I have a spot remover for the clothes I design. Would you like me to fetch it from my room?"

Gayatri replied, shoulders relaxing, "You're so kind. I'll come with you to your room."

"It's highly toxic, so it is better if I apply it directly with gloves," said Ruby. "I brewed a concentrated form in the lab in college. I wouldn't want to leave it lying about or take a risk with it. I do need to apply it right away, so why don't I go to my room to fetch it. Then I'll meet you in your room to take the dress while you change?"

"Yes. Lovely. Thank you ever so much," said Gayatri. With that, the two of them left and the party returned to its small oases of triplets scattered about the room.

Turning back to Fina and Sajida, the Earl said with the bluster of an angler casting about for a fish in the ocean, "Aubrey-Havelock. Tavistock... yes..."

Quickly cutting him off, Fina turned to Sajida and said, "I heard you've been visiting your sister at Oxford. Have you had much chance to see London?"

Sajida replied breathlessly, "Oh yes. I find Oxford a bore, so I try to travel down to London to the shops whenever possible. It's not like shopping in Paris, of course, but I did find this divine number there," she said, placing her hand on her hip.

Fina smiled and murmured her approval, not wanting to break Sajida's flow of excitement.

"I have other relatives living in London as well, so I use the excuse of seeing them," she tittered. "I hear you work with Ruby. Do you also study at Oxford? Your face looks familiar. Perhaps a party? That seems to be the only fun to be had at college."

"Yes – I'm reading history at St Jude's College, so it's possible you've seen me. Ruby is reading chemistry, even though her heart is in fashion design. She's spent time studying design in Paris and Port of Spain."

After taking a deep puff on his cigar, the Earl cut in, clearly hoping to join the conversation. "How did you meet Miss Dove? At Oxford?"

"No. We – ah – met in the halls of justice, you might say," said Fina, her eyes darting around the room like a trapped animal.

Fortunately enough for her, the dinner gong came to her rescue.

7

As she entered the dimly lit hall, Fina glanced up at the walls of the corridor. Not surprisingly, they were lined with imposing portraits of what she assumed were the ancestors of the Sykes-Duckworths. Not a happy looking clan on the whole, she thought. Fortunately, their dour countenances couldn't dampen the festive atmosphere of the gathering.

Guests trickled into the dining room, including the almost-on-time arrival of Gayatri and Ruby – formal entries were apparently eschewed at Pauncefort Hall. There were, however, place cards in gold lettering. Two seats remained conspicuously unfilled, and Fina could see storm clouds gathering on the Earl's brow as he contemplated them.

"Curse it, where are those two young—" The clatter of feet cut him off, and in came the pair of miscreants, somewhat out of breath.

Fina held her breath as she recognized the pale face and tightly trimmed moustache of Leslie-dashed-Dashwood. Thankfully, he was seated down the other end of the long table, and did not give her so much as a glance. The other young man must be Granville, favoured eldest son and heir. He certainly was handsome, thought Fina. His neatly groomed blond hair, fingernails and spotless shoes confirmed what she had seen of his personality in his bedroom. A ruthless jaw to match a ruthless personality.

Trying not to look as though she had been scrutinizing the guests, Fina eased into her chair between Cyril and Julia. Ruby, Edgar and Ian sat across from them.

Ian broke the silence – a silence that had been only punctuated by the slurping of soup. "Professor Lighton, what is your subject at Oxford? I went to the University of Havana, but I've always wanted to see Oxford."

"Politics. I am a senior lecturer in politics," replied Cyril curtly. "That usually shuts down any conversation."

Rising to the challenge, Julia said, "Ah, but to the contrary, dear Professor. I believe you may find some of us, despite appearances, are deeply interested in the political world. What is your view of the colonial occupation of Egypt?"

Cyril, his mouth full of bread roll, was able only to raise his finger in answer. Seizing his chance, Edgar glanced up from whatever had fascinated him in his lap and stammered, "What's your interest in Egypt, Miss Aston?"

"I was born in Egypt to a British father and an Egyptian mother. It was quite a scandal at the time," she said, airily waving her soup spoon. "My mother died when I was quite young. My father and I moved to England. I was shunted off to many years of boarding school. I do plan to return to Egypt at some point, but the situation there—"

At last, Cyril found himself free to break in. "That's just it. As you say, Miss Aston, it's a deplorable situation, a colonial occupation. The Egyptians must govern themselves. I am of the opinion that if the British do not leave, there will continue to be overt and covert violence against the Egyptian people. And that is intolerable. This Blueshirt and Greenshirt business only proves my point."

Crash. Plates rattled on the ivory tablecloth as Granville's hand, clutching a napkin, came down hard. "I see we have some Bolshies!" cut in Granville with a snort. "What is the rot I hear at that end of the table?" He clearly had no intention of hearing anything, thought Fina.

Edgar muttered under his breath, "Better than the r-r-rot at that end of the table..."

Fina clutched at her stomach as Edgar went back to peeling his cuticles.

"What's that, dearest Eddie? I cannot hear you! Or are you too weak to respond, as usual?" Granville taunted.

At this point, the rest of the family sallied forth in defence of Edgar: "Now dear, I don't think it is fair to treat your brother that way..." said the Countess, halting abruptly, followed by "Granville, you're squiffy," said plainly by his sister, then followed finally by the Earl "Now it doesn't do to talk politics over dinner, you two. It's Christmastime after all."

Silence.

Leslie, with surprising sensitivity, thought Fina, intervened to divert Granville's attention. "I say, Granny, what did you think of that scrum we had last week? Did you see how Gableton-Fitts caught one in the back? Rough one, that, though the referee's call was utter tosh."

Tension now broken, a collective inaudible sigh permeated the room. By mutual, unspoken consent, the guests kept the conversation safely on local matters, expressing a surprising level of interest in the nearby Holy Well, which Florence Nightingale and Charles Darwin had reportedly visited in order to take the waters.

Fighting the urge to lick the bowl of her sherry trifle, Fina distracted herself by observing – one of her favourite habits in life. Most of the guests had paired off into cosy conversations. Ian and Ruby chattered about various relatives and shared acquaintances across the Caribbean; it seemed that Ian had some connections in the Bahamas. Edgar and Cyril, meanwhile, continued to debate the continued existence of the British Empire.

"Yes, I see your point, Professor, but you must agree with Nye Bevan's argument about poverty. Surely that applies in the colonies as well."

Sniffing impatiently, like a lord who has heard the hundredth excuse from a peasant that day for the lack of grain production, Cyril said, "Bevan's time is up. His pronouncements are all very good for England, but I hardly believe they extend to the colonies. Bakunin says…"

Pompous as shop cats, thought Fina. She was tired of the Oxford habit of one-upmanship of name dropping.

Turning to Julia, she asked what she hoped would not be a rude question about her clothing. "Miss Aston, I'm so looking forward to delving into your wardrobe tomorrow. I find your use of clothes that are traditionally more, er, masculine in style intriguing. Is it your signature?"

Brushing some invisible lint off her lapel, Julia gently chided, not unkindly, "What makes you decide to wear dresses at all, darling?"

"Oh – I didn't mean…" stammered Fina.

"Forgive me – I couldn't help myself," said Julia, as she looked into her empty dish – as if it contained answers to the mysteries of the universe. "You see, I am asked that question so very often. I have a rather pat response."

"I'm sorry to join that chorus," said Fina, wrinkling her nose.

"I suppose it is my interest in clothing design that drives my question rather than any judgment. I'm sorry if it's an unfair question."

"Oh, hell," said Julia, throwing down her napkin. "What's the point of clothes if you can't have a little fun with them?" Searching her jacket pockets, she said, "Ian, do you have a ciggy? I'm fresh out."

Without taking his eyes off Ruby, Ian pulled out a box of cigarettes and slid them across the table.

"Thanks, sweetie," said Julia, winking at Ian as he gave her an almost imperceptible glance. After igniting her 'ciggy' with a mother-of-pearl lighter, she turned toward her partner on the right, Lady Charlotte.

Having clearly failed at dinner conversation, Fina settled back into her chair, ruminating about the exact nature of the relationship between Ian and Julia. She wondered if Julia were jealous. Julia had a studied insouciance about her, but she was an actress after all. Ian and Ruby were getting on like a house on fire. Ruby's hands waved as Ian leaned toward her, a sure sign of her excitement as she rarely used hand gestures to make a point.

Slap. It must be a family pastime to use napkin slapping to make a point, thought Fina. This time, it was the Countess doing the slapping. She began to move her bulk, gently side to side to gain enough momentum to vacate the chair.

"Grimston, please remove the trifle. Please tell the cook I prefer her older recipe – it was too sweet," declared the Countess.

"But, I, I was hoping for a bit more of that delicious trifle. I thought it quite tasty," protested the Earl, looking around the table for supporters.

Now standing with her fingers splayed on the tablecloth, the Countess looked ready to plan out her next military campaign.

Hmm. More to this batty Lady Snittlegarth than meets the eye, thought Fina.

"Nonsense. It will do you good to cut back on sweets, Roger," said the Countess with the tone of finality. The other women at the table popped up from their chairs, at attention. "Ladies, please follow me to the library for coffee."

8

As they turned the corner into the library, Fina gave out a little gasp.

Flashes of colour moved through clear glass orbs – some placed precariously atop towers of books around the room.

Fina blurted out "Fish!" and then felt her face warm as she said it.

No one else replied. She was grateful no one seemed to have noticed – they were apparently all transfixed by the spectacle before them. Fluttering, spinning and sashaying fish in reds, greens and blues made the room seem as if it were moving of its own accord.

The Countess traversed the precarious makeshift fish stands with ease, halting at the largest bowl in the library.

She began to murmur gibberish at the fish. The only word Fina could make out was 'Snookums', apparently the name of one of the fish. The Countess' snub nose twitched and her lips opened and closed softly as she mimicked the large scarlet fish bobbing in front of her.

Suddenly, her back moved to an upright position, like a fast-moving drawbridge. "Forgive me, dear ladies. I was carried away by my snookums. Please let me introduce you to my wonderful world of guppies, tetras and swordtails."

Looking around the room, Fina felt the warmth leaving her face – the other women's mouths opened and closed like Lady Snittlegarth's beloved snookums.

"Don't be shy, ladies. Please do have a look. Once you're finished, let us congregate near the fireplace," she said as she motioned to move her flock of women toward the crackling fire and emerald silk sofas.

Ruby and Fina eased into the corners of a sofa nearest the fireplace. Turning toward the somewhat distracted Lady Snittlegarth across from them, Ruby asked, "Is this a hobby or necessity for you, Lady Snittlegarth?"

"Please, dear, call me Alma," she said, as she gazed at the fishbowl near her shoulder. Her small, but pleasing double chin quivered with excitement.

With one deft movement, the Countess poured a bottle of orange flakes into the bowl, causing chaos among the three fish.

"Let me introduce you, Miss Dove and Miss Aubrey-Havelock," she said, without moving her gaze from the fish.

"To whom?" asked Fina.

"To the fish, of course," she said with a slightly exasperated sigh. "This is Flopsy," she said, pointing to an arrogant green guppy. "And this is Mopsy and Cottontail," pointing to the two conventional goldfish. "Now," she said, turning back to the two women. "Your question, Miss Dove. You see, I find fish and aquarium building just fascinating. I belong to the Royal Aquarium Society. I won best tropical aquarium two years in a row," she said, her eyes aglow with pleasure, "though I rarely attend the shows myself."

"And why is that, Countess?" asked Ruby, playing along.

"Why, I simply cannot enter the exhibition hall without being overcome with bufonophobia," she said.

Fina blinked.

Ruby leaned over and whispered to Fina, "Fear of toads."

Lady Snittlegarth continued on, either unworried or unaware of their exchange. "I find it a soothing task, especially in the winter when one cannot garden," she said motioning toward the window. In the darkness, Fina could just make out the soft white hummocks of snow against the panes.

Glancing at the plethora of aquarium-related titles on the oak table closest to her, Ruby motioned to the Countess with an enquiring gesture. Nodding her assent, Ruby peered at the stack of leather spines in gold and crimson. She reached for the one that read 'sugar plantation' in fading letters so that it looked like 'uga plant'. As she fingered through the volume, she asked in a calm, detached voice, "This seems an interesting topic – especially since my family is from the Caribbean. Your family has a connection, doesn't it? Lady Charlotte mentioned it when we arrived this afternoon."

The Countess' engaging smile transformed precipitously from genuine to false. She began to twist her wedding ring compulsively. "Ah – yes, of course. You must know about Lavington's in St Kitts. Granville will become senior member in the company soon. After his upcoming graduation at Oxford. I am hopeful he will steer the proverbial ship in the correct direction."

"I'm afraid I'm not much up on international finance," said Ruby. Fina saw a well-worn expression of false-innocence appear on Ruby's face. "Has Lavington's had some trouble?" Ruby picked up the warm cup of coffee and cradled it between the palms of her hands.

Fina sensed that she might be cramping Ruby's style. "Will you excuse me? Gayatri looks lonely," she said in a conspiratorial whisper. Scooping up her cup, Fina retired to Gayatri's sofa.

This piece of furniture had the added benefit of being close enough to still overhear the Countess and Ruby.

"Well, I don't pretend to understand the vagaries of global trade in sugar cane," said the Countess, waving her hand in the air. "I do know that something went very wrong, but I assume it must be some sort of internal management problem. Henry mentioned it in passing when he came home last year. Or perhaps a bad season?" she asked, as if Ruby could supply her with an answer.

Fina could see her friend fighting the urge to provide the suspected answer. Ruby said airily, "I expect that must be it. I do know that there—"

Interrupting Ruby as if she had finally landed on the correct formulaic answer, the Countess said hurriedly, "Of course, it must be that horrid competition – what's-it-called? Dulcet & Sons. Yes, that's it. They've caused poor Henry no end of trouble. Dulcet used to have an iron grip on the sugar industry there, but lately they've been expanding their trade into other areas and other stocks. I just hope they spread themselves too thin and go under this year."

Before she could stop herself, Fina cast a quick look of enlightenment at Ruby. So those papers she'd found in Edgar's room were a report on Lavington's competition! Compiled without Dulcet's knowledge or cooperation, presumably. But they were still no closer to finding out why the list of assets and debts had had such a strong effect on the reader.

Pausing a moment as if she had let the cat out of the bag, the Countess pounced on her coffee and swiftly gulped it as if it were a reviving brandy. Hinting that she had provided quite enough information for the moment, she changed the subject to couture. "I'm afraid I'm not particularly fashionable, Miss Dove. Do tell me what you think of Paris this year."

Across the way, Fina drained one cup of coffee and then

another. The champagne had been potent and she knew she had a long night ahead. Gayatri sat impassive, her back ramrod-straight, making no attempt at conversation. She had not spoken a word since they had entered the library, apart from requesting a cup of Assam tea from Grimston. Even the fish, which had Julia in raptures, had failed to thaw her reserve.

Thinking about the origin of the phrase 'tension so thick you could cut it with a knife', Fina grasped for a distracting topic.

"Miss Badarur, did Ruby's stain remover succeed in clearing up that splotch on your lovely gown?"

"Oh yes, Miss Aubrey-Havelock. And please do call me Gayatri. Well, it worked a treat, as our cook would say. I must see about getting some for myself. Do you think Miss Dove would lend me the recipe?"

"I'm afraid it is unlikely," said Fina apologetically. "And please do call me Fina. It is a special concentrate made from… what is it? Oxalic acid – highly toxic, so she doesn't even let me use it. She has made all sorts of concoctions in the lab that are not only stain removers, but richly hued dyes."

"Really? I must make an appointment to see her," she said with her eyebrows raised. "Or, I should say that Sajida should make an appointment, since she is the shopper in our family," she added, gesturing toward her sister. Sajida lounged, rather than sat, idly admiring her impeccably manicured, scarlet nails.

Responding with a knowing smile, Fina asked, "So you must be here because of your Oxford connection?"

"Oh–I–hmm. Was it Granville or Edgar who asked us down?" she said, more to herself. She fiddled with the curl of hair at the back of her neck. She looked over at Sajida for a rescue, but Sajida continued her stupendous act of nonchalance, casting a bored stare at one of the fishbowls.

Gayatri gave a quick smile, as if to ease the embarrassment. "Oh, yes, that's it. Actually, though I know Granville and Edgar as acquaintances, Professor Lighton made the formal invitation on behalf of Edgar, once he heard that my sister would be visiting from India. It's such a wonderful chance for us to learn the old English customs, you see." She waved a delicate hand around the library, taking in the holly that draped the shelves. "I also know Ian, as well as one does in London and Oxford..." Gayatri trailed off nervously. Fina noticed that her eyes dilated when she mentioned Ian's name, so she assumed her temporary loss of words was due to attraction – rather than nefarious activities.

"And you – what's your connection? You're also at Oxford?" enquired Gayatri, recovering by sitting more upright in the over-stuffed sofa.

"Yes, and I've heard of Granville and Edgar, as one does," Fina said, unconsciously mimicking Gayatri's earlier words. "Granville has quite the reputation, doesn't he?" she said in a conspiratorial hush, hoping this would prompt a bit of gossip.

"Oh yeesss," Gayatri said with a knowing smile. "*People* love him. I cannot think why. I've also heard he loses a lot at the roulette table. I don't know how he gets through his studies at all. I guess that's what being a son of empire does for you," she said, nearly spitting out the words.

There was a soft cough. Fina turned to see that Grimston had sidled up to the sofa. His eyelids flickered impassively at Lady Snittlegarth.

"Yes," said the Countess, looking up from her coffee. "What is it, Grimston?"

"The gentlemen have retired to the saloon, milady, and await your company. They are moving to that room because it has a... piano," said Grimston, grimacing at the mention of the instrument as if it were a distasteful guest.

"Yes, yes, Grimston. A piano doesn't bite."

"No, milady."

"Ladies!" announced the Countess, sleeves fluttering again as she struggled from the sofa, grateful for Grimston's proffered hand of assistance.

"If you'd be so kind as to follow me to the saloon. Roger wanted to have the piano in here, you know, but I told him it simply wouldn't do. My poor fish do not abide by vibrations. I'm afraid it gives them a dreadful headache," she clucked.

9

With heads bent together like schoolgirls, Ruby and Fina quickly traded notes in the dimly lit hallway.

"Did you hear what she said about Dulcet?" said Fina.

"I did!" said Ruby. "There's something odd going on there, no doubt. And I'd bet my life Granville is involved somehow."

"Yes... you know, I didn't like the look of him one bit, now I see him up close. And as for his friend!"

Ruby pitched her voice even lower. "Charlotte doesn't seem too fond of Leslie Dashwood, either. I remarked to her earlier that he looked somewhat ill – perhaps his spleen – and she told me she suspects he may be troubled in his mind. We'd be best advised to steer clear of him this weekend, she said."

"That's one piece of advice I'm delighted to take," said Fina fervently as they neared the saloon. "And let me tell you about Gayatri..."

Just then, a dark-coated figure nearly collided with them.

"So sorry – oh, it's you, Charles! Why are you in a serving uniform? Were you at dinner and we didn't see you?" asked Ruby.

"I... They... They're short-staffed, you see, as many of the servants couldn't make it in this weather. I served dinner and then attended the gentlemen in the study."

"I'm ashamed that I looked right past you at dinner," said Fina, feeling the warmth creeping up her neck for what felt like the thousandth time that day. Why was she nervous? "Will you be able to listen to the music in the saloon?"

Ruby interjected, "Doesn't Ian count songwriting among his many talents? I heard Julia is also quite a nightingale."

Glancing over his shoulder, presumably to ensure the omnipresent Grimston wasn't lurking in the shadows, Charles responded in a whisper. "I should be able to stand out in the hall to listen, if not to watch. Grimston has to have his cigarettes or he gets moody," he said, waving Ruby and Fina into the saloon.

As their eyes adjusted to the bright combination of electric and candlelight of the room, Fina noticed both Granville and Leslie were absent. The saloon was a long room with French windows at one end and a gleaming grand piano at the other. The guests were arranged – much like a stage play or a painting, thought Fina – around the mantel, sofas and small bridge table in the corner. Julia looked pensive. She lounged in the corner, smoking a cigarette; it was hardly the stance of a joyful singer. Fina noticed her fierce glare at Ian and Gayatri who were cosily ensconced in the corner. Despite their hushed conversation, Gayatri's tinkling laugh floated across the room, as if it were a butterfly in search of an exit. In response, Julia stubbed out her cigarette in a bronze ashtray with striking ferocity. She marched over to Ian and Gayatri.

"Here comes trouble," hissed Ruby. They made a beeline for the nearest sofa with a view of the brewing tempest.

Hands on hips, Julia said, "Ian, may I speak to you for a moment? Alone." She glared at Gayatri.

With a sensitivity heretofore hidden beneath the rather

superficial surface, Sajida jumped up and zipped over to her sister's rescue. "Gay," she said – pronouncing her sister's pet name as *guy* – "I simply must ask you about Mother's letter from today." She opened her scarlet clutch and proffered the crumpled letter to her sister, while guiding her gently away from the smouldering Julia.

Ian, looking somewhat sheepish, made his escape to the piano.

Julia followed. She removed her blazer with the flourish of a matador – an effect heightened, Fina thought, by the pool of black satin lining that flashed as she tossed it on the nearest armchair. With deliberate insouciance, she undulated toward the piano, no small feat given her beanpole figure. Smoothing her hair and her blouse, she pursed her lips and leaned over the piano to whisper to Ian. Almost imperceptibly, Ian shrank like a frightened turtle from Julia. Whatever the conversation was, it was rather curt.

Wondering if these developing love triangles would affect their mission this weekend, Fina studied her friend in the next chair. Ruby sat, hands gently folded in her lap, gazing at the piano. Or, to be more precise, at Ian. Selkies and kelpies, thought Fina. While she was happy for Ruby – perhaps a teensy jealous – she hoped this infatuation wouldn't distract her from gathering tidbits of gossip about the other guests. Infatuation. Hmph. She found herself glancing at Charles.

Charles topped up the guests' drinks while they arranged themselves to pay appropriate attention to the music. The Earl raised his cut glass tumbler for Scotch, and then turned his attention to the piano. In a slightly slurred but contented voice, he said, "Play us a Christmas tune, by Jove!" Nimble on his feet, Charles dodged the Earl's sloshing glass as he began to swing it in anticipation of the music.

Smirking slightly with urbane distaste, Ian nodded to Julia.

They launched into a lively rendition of a song Fina hadn't heard before, but it had the refrain 'Santa Claus is coming to town'. A crimson-faced Earl grinned and hummed along – though clearly it was to a tune in his own head. The Countess patted her husband's arm with a gesture that could have been interpreted as either condescending or encouraging, while Charlotte tried to ignore her uncle by staring at her apparently rather fascinating champagne glass. Other guests listened attentively – though it was a bit too serious, thought Fina, for the rather frivolous tune.

As polite applause broke out at the close of the song, Granville and Leslie stumbled in – with cigarettes escaping at gravity-defying angles from their mouths and tumblers free of liquid. Despite this, Fina thought Granville must be relatively sober, given that he had left his wineglass more or less untouched throughout dinner. *Relatively*. This was in sharp contrast to his friend who, as she knew all too well, had been on a strict diet of liquid calories since the afternoon.

"Ripping, absolutely ripping," slurred Leslie, as he saluted the musical entertainment in the corner. Unable to balance all of his various accoutrements, he let his cigarette slip out of his mouth and onto the lap of Gayatri who was now sitting near the door.

Granville snorted with the undisguised glee of a drunk. Charlotte's eyes were wide with horror as Gayatri quickly brushed off her second dress of the night. Sajida leapt up and rushed at Leslie. *Slap*. An angry red flush spread across Leslie's face. She glared at him, saying nothing. Turning around like a soldier at the palace, she moved to tend to her sister.

Charles swooped over to Leslie to pull him away. "Please, sir, why don't I get you another drink and find a seat for you – over here," he said, gesturing to two chairs facing one another in the nether regions of the saloon.

Leslie stiffened, as if determined to kick his inebriation by sheer force of will. He and Granville allowed themselves to be installed in a corner obscured from Fina's vision by a large mahogany chest.

Ruby grabbed Fina's arm and whispered, "Did you see that? That slap was for more than that drunken accident."

Fina nodded and grimaced in response as the next song commenced at the behest of the Countess, who was quick to return to the veneer of normalcy.

As apparent rapt attention was expected given their proximity to the performance, Fina's face stayed fixed, while her mind wandered. There certainly was an atmosphere. And this atmosphere only made her more anxious. She was anxious to begin their search tonight. She was anxious that she would fail in her task and fail her friend. Fina reminded herself that they were in this together, and that she should stop putting Ruby on a pedestal. As her anxieties began to overtake her, she rose and wandered to the French windows.

As she passed by Granville and Leslie, giving them as wide a berth as possible, she heard a few snippets of their conversation. The strong smell of sour Scotch wafted over her as she tried to look casually out the window.

Granville said, "You know I'll back you up, old chap."

"Yes, but this whole Parliament business has left me unsettled. And that don – if he gets wind of this, not to mention the press..." responded Leslie.

"We'll be leaving soon. Everything will be sorted out," said Granville in a surprisingly soothing voice.

Good, she thought, I hope the scoundrels will be leaving soon.

Self-conscious about her position at the window – in case anyone was watching – she decided to look longingly out the window. She saw the delicate layers of cotton-like snow gently pressing against the lower panes. And still the flakes kept falling. There would be no chance of anyone arriving or leaving tomorrow morning, and perhaps not the morning after. She shivered as she thought about her mission for the night ahead.

10

"Fina? Are you decent?" Ruby tapped lightly on the adjoining door.

"Yes, yes, do come in!"

Ruby entered and collapsed with a sigh in the nearest over-stuffed armchair. "Ahhh..." she said as she peeled her feet out of her evening shoes. "These heels are my favourite, but they certainly are not meant for long evenings... I thought the evening would never end!"

"So did I," mumbled Fina as she munched on a roll – one she had pilfered unobtrusively at dinner.

"Where did you get that roll? I'm ravenous. I couldn't eat much at dinner," Ruby said, patting her stomach sadly.

"No, you were too busy chatting up Mr Clavering, darling," said Fina in a teasing voice. "Too scrumptious for words!"

"Oh pish." One corner of Ruby's mouth lifted. It then gave way to a full smile. "He is rather dashing, isn't he?" Shaking her head and slapping her hands against her thighs, she added, "But enough of that, we have work to do!" She hesitated. "Is the kitchen on that map of places to investigate? I could really investigate the inside of a larder right now."

"I don't think it's on our list, but I suppose we could sneak down for some cocoa before or after our investigation of the other rooms. In fact, that could be our excuse if we are discovered during our search – we're looking for a book to read and a cup of cocoa before bed."

Ruby nodded. "Let's begin. I think we should go together to each room and then to the kitchen. It will look less suspicious if we're caught slinking around together rather than in separate rooms."

Slipping into the highly unfashionable but practical plimsolls Ruby had procured for the two of them, they crept down the staircase. Perhaps this was the key to Ruby's grace, thought Fina. Wear the right shoes and then it's a snap...

"Oof," said Fina as she tripped on the beautiful carpet fringe on the landing. She caught herself by grasping the railing.

"Are you all right, Feens?"

"Yes, yes," said Fina, wincing as she straightened her right ankle. "I'll be fine."

"Don't go all stoic on me, Fina," said Ruby in her best governess voice.

"No, no, I'm fine. Besides, it takes my mind off the anxiety."

They continued down the stairs without further mishaps. Fina had the same sensation she had as a child, sneaking down the staircase to see if Father Christmas had arrived. The smell, decorations and sense of danger all heightened the memory. Suddenly, she had an overwhelming urge to giggle. Must be giddy from the excitement, she thought. She suppressed the urge successfully by staring at the eerie portraits of those glum ancestors in the long gallery. Stopping at one rather imposing portrait of a man with his hand on the globe, she looked into his disturbed – perhaps even deranged – eyes. Must be the inbreeding.

Ruby gave a jump next to her as a figure emerged out of the

gloom, coming from the direction of the study. Judging by the height and hunched shoulders, it had to be Cyril. He carried a half-full brandy snifter in his hand, which he waved in their direction as he passed. Mumbling something that sounded like "grmph" under his breath, they smiled as he passed, halting their progress in case he wanted to talk. Barely acknowledging their presence, he scurried up the stairs. As touchy as a weasel, thought Fina. They continued to creep down the corridor.

Fina froze. Cocking her head to the side, she strained to hear. She could hear a gurgle of voices, not too far away. The voices were not moving toward them, nor were they fading in the distance. Ruby pointed a finger toward the study and the two moved in concert toward the entrance. With their backs flattened against the wall near the entrance, they listened.

Fina could recognize Edgar's voice. "Dash it, Granville, you, you promised... You said you'd made all the arrangements last time you spoke to old Sykes at the bank. Now you tell me you're planning to withdraw the funds?"

"Sorry, old boy," retorted Granville, his voice dripping with sarcasm. "I guess you'll have to find some other way to fund your Bolshie ideas. I'm certainly not going to help you."

A pause. Then Edgar's voice broke the silence. "I know what you did, Granville."

At the sound of a glass slamming the table, Ruby and Fina sucked in their diaphragms. Fina hoped they might melt into the background of the tapestries on the wall. Edgar stormed out of the room, nearly tripping over the long rug as he made his exit.

Fortunately for Ruby and Fina, he headed toward the stairs. After what felt to be an eternity to Fina – but was surely just a few minutes – she could hear the smacking of lips after what must have been his final drink. Granville sauntered out of the room, nearly empty snifter in hand. He hesitated in the doorway.

With her heart in her throat, she was relieved to see the flicker of
a flame, lighting up a cigarette. Swinging the hand with the
cigarette at his side, he lumbered in a hushed, inky darkness
toward the stairway.

Waving Fina on toward the study, Ruby tiptoed down the
corridor. Fina knew it wasn't necessary as they were in their cat-
burglar plimsolls, but it felt natural as they crept into the
comforting murkiness of the study. Anaemic moonlight filtered
in, reflecting a blueish light from the blanket of snow outside
the bank of windows facing west. Fina moved anti-clockwise
from the door, while Ruby made her way to the right. Their task
was intimidating; the room was packed with books from floor to
ceiling.

Grr... Fina stopped and listened. She squinted through the
gloom and saw Ruby pointing at her own stomach. Fina
responded by pulling down her lip in an exaggerated 'I'm sorry'
expression. All the more reason to speed through their task, she
thought.

Two large desks stood next to three cabinets, along with a
line-up of bookshelves. Fina decided to begin with the desks,
but the drawers were locked, apart from one which held nothing
but a broken pen-nib, a half-full bottle of Indian ink, a silver hip
flask (empty) and a race book for the previous year's Goodwood.
She moved on to the cherrywood cabinets. Nothing of interest.
Peering over at the tall bookshelf next to the cabinet – stuffed as
if it were its own jumble sale – she felt overwhelmed. She took
out a book at random and opened it, releasing a dank, mouldy
odour. Dark spots blotted the page. She put it back and took
another, only to find it equally afflicted. These books must have
been left unread for decades. They made a perfect hiding place
– too perfect, she thought ruefully. How would she and Ruby
ever get through them all?

Summoning all her strength, Fina decided to adopt a more

analytical approach. Scanning the titles, she selected 'Colonial Administration' and shook it gingerly. She performed the same operation with 'West Indies Flora and Fauna'. Finally, she came to 'Sugar Cane Production'. Bingo! A thick, yellowish envelope marked 'Bluegate' was wedged in the book jacket, hidden from prying eyes – or so someone had thought.

Adrenaline, already pumping through her veins, gave her such a rush that she felt temporarily immobile. But she managed to give a rather feeble wave – under the circumstances – of her quarry at Ruby.

Before Ruby could react, a faint scraping sound caught their ears, followed by an oddly soft thud. Without even looking at one another, the pair fled the study, away from the direction of the sound. Scurrying down the corridor to the right, they escaped down the stairs to the kitchen.

11

In the midst of gleaming copper pots and pans, Fina and Ruby heaved a sigh in unison. They collapsed at the enormous table-cum-workspace. In a quiet, but no longer hushed voice, Fina said, "I feel so much more comfortable here. More like home." Nodding her agreement, Fina could tell Ruby felt the same way by her relaxed shoulders.

Scanning the worktops, Fina's eyes alighted on a plate of cheese – Stilton? It looked inviting. The smell of dinner rolls wafted nearby.

"Let's eat and then talk," said Fina, pouncing on the cheese and rolls. They were both so engrossed in the food that they failed to hear approaching footsteps behind them.

"And just what do you think you're doing, young ladies?" said a thin woman with wispy blond-grey hair, wrapped in a tight bun. Fina noticed how her muscular forearms were out of keeping with her slight frame. Only one reason for that, she thought. This must be the cook.

Cheeks stuffed like a chipmunk's, Ruby and Fina stared at her in silence, unable to talk out of sheer physical inability rather than surprise.

In between munches, Fina said, "We're guests here at the Hall. I'm Fina and this is Ruby," gesturing to her friend. "We were peckish after a lively dinner so we thought we'd make some cocoa. But then we saw this food and couldn't help ourselves."

"Hmpf. That's what the bell pulls are for in your rooms, miss – tug on them and ask for a cocoa to be brought up to you. That's why I'm here, even though it's awfully late for Master Granville to be asking for cocoa. I already had two other guests come downstairs to get a cup of cocoa on their own." The woman's arched eyebrows showed what she thought of the younger generation.

Fina said, "I'm so sorry we interrupted your routine. Are you the cook?"

"What do you think? That I'm Lady of the Manor?" she said sarcastically, dropping a curtsey in jest. "Yes, I am. Mabel Lynn's the name," she sniffed, peering more closely at Ruby.

"Mrs Lynn," said Ruby hastily, "Are you by chance related to Nancy Lynn of Malvern? She's my mother's cousin by marriage."

Visibly thawing upon hearing this news, Mabel replied with alacrity, "Why yes, miss. She's my brother's girl. Smart one she is. Always talking about travelling somewhere, though she doesn't have two shillings to rub together. Still, I expect she'll make her way in the world. Got ambition, she has."

Now sensing the bond between them could and should be repaired, Mabel turned to a small cupboard near them. She pulled out a wedge of what looked to be a moist seed cake. "Here, have some of this. It's my specialty," she said with eagerness. She cut two generous slices, rummaged around for some forks, and served up the plates with a smile.

Making appropriate noises over the delectable morsels before them, Fina and Ruby watched the cook heat up the pan of cocoa on the range.

Half speaking to herself, she said, "This is the last of the cocoa I've made for tonight. Those young folk who came earlier took most of it. Insisted on serving themselves, they did. If you'd like any yourselves, you'll need to make it yourself," she said, gesturing to the tin of cocoa on the dresser. "I need to take this up to the master." She finished her preparations, bid them goodnight and left them to enjoy their seed cake.

"Mmm..." said Ruby. "This is scrumptious. I feel so much better now. Let's take a look at our loot from the study!"

Rubbing her hands together to scrape off the crumbs, Fina extracted the envelope from her dress pocket. With shaking hands, she slid the contents of the envelope on to the table. The small but neat handwriting on the first page read, 'Testimony of Sergeant Trace, 17 July 1933'.

Ruby squeezed her friend's arm in excitement. "This is it, Fina! Well done. Let's read it quickly and then take a look at what I found."

I, Sergeant James Ronald Trace, hereby swear the following testimony is true to the best of my knowledge.

On 15 July 1933, I was at my post at Lavington's sugar plantation at Bluegate. I witnessed a group of twenty sugar plantation workers gather to bring their demands for better conditions to the owners of Lavington's Sugar Company. Though I did not know their explicit demands, I had heard rumours that workers had been trying to gather support for better conditions. My post was positioned near the offices of Lavington's so I could see approximately twenty workers approach. They entered the Lavington's and left ten minutes later. The workers did not look pleased. Young Master Granville exited the office after them and yelled something that I could not understand – though I had a clear view of the situation, I was far enough away that I could not hear the precise words, though they were undoubtedly hostile.

While this interaction was a highly unusual occurrence, I went back to my duties, especially as I was the only one on guard that day. Perhaps an hour later, I heard a series of gunshots, coming from the direction of the cane fields. I took my rifle and ran to the fields. As I approached, I could see a figure riding off down the track, with a gun resting on the pommel. I cannot identify the figure, but the horse was the bay from Lavington's stables.

The scene when I arrived was horrific. Ten of the workers had been shot – I recognized most of them to be part of the group that had visited the offices earlier. When I asked the witnesses to tell me who had committed this crime, they fell silent. I could see the fear in their eyes. I did come across a young boy, however, who told me that it was 'the white bosses' who shot the workers, though his mother hushed him as soon as she saw him talking to me.

When I confronted the owners of Lavington's in the office that day, they denied all involvement, including the fact that they had met with the workers earlier that day. I wrote a full account and submitted it to my senior officers. I heard nothing from them, but a week later I was told that I was no longer needed in St Kitts and that I would be reassigned to another post.

I write this account as a form of protection for myself, should anything happen to me. I also write it for those who died. I can acknowledge that though I did my duty in reporting the massacre to my superiors, I am terrified of what will happen to me if I do tell my story to the British press.

As she reached the end, Fina felt her throat close up. Though the testimony in the document was hardly news, it was stomach-churning to read. She did not have Ruby's direct connection, but she knew enough colonial history to recognize familiar patterns of violence. Glancing at her friend, she saw the tears welling in her eyes as she read.

Rubbing her temples, Fina said gently, "I know it's horrific. But it's what we've been looking for. Let's cheer up."

Silence.

Quickly realizing her mistake from Ruby's glare, she amended, "I'm sorry. I shouldn't try to pretend this isn't emotional – and make it seem all right." Though they sat in silence, it was a companionable silence, staring at the paper.

"I'll be all right. Remembering our purpose makes it easier." Ruby sniffed and wiped away her tears. "Give me the paper and I'll make sure it stays somewhere safe."

"Not back in the study?"

"I don't think I can face going back in there tonight, especially after that strange noise."

They padded up the stairs wearily to their rooms. Promising to wake early to discuss further plans, they bid each other a good night.

12

Fina blinked in the dim morning glow. The sunlight – though she felt that was a strong word to use – was obscured by the gently falling snow at the window. She wriggled her toes, savouring the warmth of the feather eiderdown and the plush, deep pillow. Maybe just five more minutes, she thought. Unusually enough for her, however, that delicious slightly-conscious drifting did not materialize. Her nose felt cold; with the staff shortage, no housemaid had crept in to light her bedroom fire, and the room was icy.

She ruminated on the previous night's adventures. As she was wont to do, she ran the story about her faux pas with Ruby over and over again. Fina reflected that she sometimes felt like a much younger sister to Ruby – someone who had accomplished so much in her life already. Deep down, Fina also knew that she did not want to be like one of *those* people, like Granville, or like really anyone in the house. She also knew that it was impossible to separate herself, the daughter of an earl, from them.

Gently chiding herself for wandering off like a lost puppy in her brain, she prepared herself for the day to come. What would they do now that they had essentially accomplished their task?

Had they been too successful? Would Granville or others in the family discover that the papers had disappeared? Who would take the papers from Ruby – and what in heaven's name would they do with them?

A soft knock at the door interrupted her reverie. "Yes, come in," Fina croaked.

Ruby slipped in, stylish, as always, in her soft mauve-coloured dressing gown. She hopped onto the edge of the bed and patted Fina's feet with a playful touch. Fina let out a small sigh of relief.

Invigorated by her friend's encouragement, Fina sat up as if she were a garden rake that had been trodden upon. "Hmm... I wonder what's for breakfast? I'm starving!"

"I hope there's plenty of toast and eggs. I could murder some bacon, too," responded Ruby.

"And pots and pots of strong tea and coffee!" rejoined Fina.

Fina peered out the window as she cinched the tie on her dressing gown.

"Good lord, there's feet and feet of snow. I believe we're officially snowed in," said Fina as she clapped her hands like a child, remembering that it was Christmastime.

"Yes, I like snow, too, but this means if we need to make our escape early – because we had a successful search – then we won't be able to... but I cannot think about anything until I've eaten and had some tea," groaned Ruby.

After they had bathed and dressed, the two friends tripped lightly down the stairs. As they came to a halt at bottom of the stairs, Grimston piloted them to breakfast in the dining room.

The smell that enveloped them made their stomachs grumble fiercely. Lifting silver-clad lids revealed a plentiful breakfast of poached and fried eggs, sausage, slices of thick bacon, grilled kidneys, fried and toasted bread, potatoes and kippers along the sideboard. Damning the constraints of supposed lady-like eating – especially as there was no one there to notice – they piled their plates high with food. Fina began with piping hot coffee and cream, while Ruby filled her cup with tea.

Fina snapped her napkin with a flourish before settling it on her lap. They ate in a companionable silence, broken only by the scrape of forks, tapping of teaspoons and the comforting sound of teacups placed in their saucers. Once their stomachs had been placated, they began to discuss plans for the day.

"I'll need to finish the design consultation with Lady Charlotte at some point today, if not tomorrow," said Ruby, flipping through the small sketchbook she always had with her. "Then I think we'll need to start one with Julia as well. At least that's what she told me last night."

"I'm afraid I might have offended Julia last night with my probing questions about her penchant for masculine dress," said Fina, feeling relieved by sharing her awkward moment with someone.

"Darling Feens, you can be a bit straight-laced sometimes," said Ruby with a smile. "Still, Julia seems to be the type of person who probably wouldn't be fazed by such a comment. Please do come with me. I need your expert advice on fit and colour."

Fina felt flattered by this comment. Her curves and hips – and meagre clothes budget – meant she had spent time designing clothes to fit her figure.

Feeling permission to continue to feed her curves, Fina expertly slathered marmalade on a small square of toast. "What do we do about the testimony? What if Granville – or whoever hid it – finds out the testimony is missing?"

Ruby dabbed the corners of her mouth with her napkin before carefully smoothing it on her lap. Leaning over in a conspiratorial manner, she said, "That's just a risk we'll have to take. I know what I've got to do with it, but it's too soon; we'll have to sit tight."

"Yes – even if someone discovers that it is missing, they cannot accuse any of the guests, or even reveal that it's gone, because then they'd have to reveal the contents of the testimony," said Fina, feeling pleased that the coffee had stimulated her grey cells – a term borrowed from a detective novel she had recently procured at a local bookshop.

Ruby smiled, reading her mind. "I see that we've both had our morning dose of caffeine. Let's make best use of it by returning to the study. I've had an idea, and we need to do a little research... unnoticed, preferably."

"Bother. All the way back to the study!" said Fina. She could barely move under the weight of her stomach. She loved a hearty breakfast, but even she had to admit that was excessive.

Winking at her, Ruby pushed back her chair, and they ambled, or rather waddled, out of the room.

13

In the grey snow-obscured daylight, Fina felt the study was surprisingly more ominous than the previous evening. The heavy dark furniture – crammed around the room – reminded her of an auction house rather than a study. Ruby made a beeline for the bookshelf by the desk.

"Help me find an atlas," she said over her shoulder. "Any one will do." They scanned the shelves together until they found a *Harmsworth's Atlas of the World* from 1920. By the cracking noise it made when she opened it, it hadn't seen much use. Ruby flipped to the back, scanning the index pages with her finger until she came to the letter N.

"That's it!" she exclaimed in a whisper. "Nowgong is a city in north-eastern India."

Fina blinked. Ruby was looking at her expectantly. "Er... quite," she said, feeling that her little grey cells were letting her down. "But what does that have to do with the Sykes-Duckworths?"

"Nowgong – *Now* – on the financial report you found in Edgar's room, remember? That wasn't a call to action; it was a note of where Dulcet & Sons owned property worthy of interest."

"Yes, there was something in the report about properties. But surely there's no sugar cane in India."

"No, but Nowgong is in Assam. And the Dulcet property that Edgar was so interested in is very likely to be a plantation."

"A plantation? Of course – Assam – tea!" said Fina, light beginning to dawn.

"Charlotte mentioned the family had plantations elsewhere. I was puzzled because I knew that the plantation in St Kitts was the only one they owned in the Caribbean. Then I began to wonder if she meant some other sort of plantation. When I hear the word plantation, I usually think of sugar or cotton, but it obviously applies to tea as well. That's why I wanted to check on the name," said Ruby as she snapped the atlas shut.

Fina's eyes glowed as she remembered the conversation she had yesterday. "Sajida is visiting from Tezpur. Isn't that a city in Assam as well?"

"I think so, but let's be sure," she said, as pages flew past her fingers to the letter T. "Yes. You're absolutely right."

"Surely there must be a connection. Do you suppose that Sajida's family is somehow linked to Dulcet? She is a princess, after all, and her family must own land in Assam."

"It's an idea," said Ruby thoughtfully. "They could be here to facilitate some sort of deal. But does it ring true to you? I'd say it doesn't square with the attitudes of Gayatri and Sajida. If anything, they seemed rather hostile to the family in the library last night."

Recalling Gayatri's stiff posture on the sofa, Fina was inclined to agree. There had been a tension there that had nothing to do with the chit-chat about Paris fashions. And Gayatri had been remarkably vague about her reasons for spending Christmas here, in the deep countryside, so far from her usual glittering London society circle.

Fina's mind suddenly flew to the Bluegate testimony. If Gayatri and her sister had links to Dulcet & Sons, anything that worked against Lavington's would be immensely valuable to them. There was an even a chance that they were Ruby's mysterious contacts, the ones who had promised that the papers would be used to root out injustice if only they were in the right hands.

If that was the case, Fina thought, no wonder Ruby hadn't wanted to say much about it on the train. The involvement of 'foreign-born aristocrats' in a plot to bring down a perfectly respectable and profitable English business, run by an Earl, would be headline news indeed.

"Do you think all this has anything to do with the argument we overheard last night?" she asked, hoping to change the subject.

Ruby tapped her teeth – a sure sign she was deep in thought. "I shouldn't think so," she said at last. "But it certainly complicates the situation."

Fina wandered about the room, checking the corners that had been too dark to see last night. She glanced down to her right at the French windows, where the snow was pleading to be let in to warm itself by the fire. That's odd, she thought, noticing a rug with a large discoloration by the doors. She trod on it tentatively, and it gave a slight spongy squelching sound, indicating it was wet. Maybe there was a leak in the door and the snow melted? Surely no one could have entered given the height of the snowfall.

"Ruby?" said Fina, motioning over to French windows.

"Hmm..." said Ruby, who was bent over a bookshelf, unable to see Fina's hand gestures.

"Can you come over here? There's something strange."

Ruby padded over to the French windows and frowned at the dark spot. "That is odd. It looks as though someone opened the doors from the inside. No one could come in from the outside, with all that snow."

"But I'm sure it wasn't here last night. I might not have seen it, but I would have felt it." She traded an anxious glance with Ruby. "Do you suppose someone came in here after we did?"

"Wouldn't we have heard something?"

"Not from the kitchen. But do you remember that curious noise, a sort of scraping? What if there was someone nearby... and they heard us?"

Ruby, normally so serene, looked apprehensive. "Perhaps we left here just in time."

There was a tense silence as the two considered the implications. "I don't like it in this room," said Fina with a shiver. "Let's leave."

14

In the hallway, Fina saw Charles scurrying about like a crab just let out of a barrel, unsure of where to go or what to do. She noticed that his shoulders were hunched and brow furrowed. Ruby, obviously noticing the same, approached him and queried, "Are you all right, Charles? Is something wrong?"

He jumped. "Oh, pardon me, I'm so sorry, Miss Dove, I didn't see the two of you there. Good morning to you both."

He hesitated.

As this was clearly going to be a guessing game, Fina prompted, "Is it about the snow? I imagine it presents a problem for you and the staff this morning." Even as she said this, she knew that it must be something more serious than the weather.

"No," he retorted. "It's, it's Master Granville, Miss Aubrey-Havelock. Mary, the maid, brings his coffee up to him every morning – when he is in residence at the Hall, of course – at nine o'clock. On the dot. He becomes quite agitated if it is not brought up precisely at nine. It serves as a type of wake-up call, I guess you might say," he said, running his hands through his dark hair. They were trembling.

Ruby went over and put a kind hand on his shoulder.

"Charles, do you want to sit down?" Indeed, thought Fina, he looked as though he had food poisoning. A high yellow sheen of sweat covered his face.

"Thank you, Miss Dove. I'm fine," he said, taking in a deep gulp of rejuvenating air. "Well, as I was saying, this morning, Mary knocked and knocked at his door and there was no answer. I saw her on the staircase on her way down to tell someone. It wasn't that I didn't believe her, honestly, but I thought I'd try myself. No answer. Complete silence, even as I put my ear up to the door – not that you can hear much through those solid oak doors."

"Have you told anyone else?" asked Ruby. "Can we help?"

"That's kind of you, Miss Dove. I was on my way to find Grimston to consult with him," he said, shifting his body in the opposite direction.

"Ah, I see. Well, we've already breakfasted and are ready to start the day. We'll meet you near Granville's room to see if we can be of any assistance," she said as he began to back away.

Fina turned to Ruby. "Granville had quite a bit to drink last night – that must be it, don't you agree?"

"Yes. Although by the quantity he consumed, my guess is that he does this quite regularly," replied Ruby. "We don't have much to do until the others have breakfasted, so shall we make our way to his room?"

Soon after they arrived, Charles, Grimston, the Earl and Mary joined them in the hallway outside Granville's impressive door. Grimston rapped on the door, and by the grimace on his face, this was surely something he had never done in his many years at Pauncefort Hall. "Sir, are you awake, sir? Can you hear me? Sir—"

"See here, Grimston, I'll give it a go," said the Earl, pounding with all his might. "Wake up, m'boy!"

Silence.

"I already tried the door with a key, sir," said Mary, twisting her apron, "but it must be bolted from the inside. I did the same with the side door through the bathroom, but it's bolted as well."

The Earl, already florid by nature, turned crimson from the effort exerted on the door. "Let's break it down!" he said, leaning heavily against the oak panelling to catch his breath.

"Ahem," coughed Charles, confidently. "Lord Snittlegarth, shall we try to break down the bathroom door? I believe it is considerably thinner than the bedroom door."

"Ah, yes, Charles. Lead the way," said the Earl.

Charles and Grimston made quick work of the door, knocking it from its hinges. The rather nervous party filed into the narrow, immaculate bathroom. Charles and Grimston took turns hurling their bulk against the mahogany door of the adjoining bedroom until it finally gave way.

Despite her curiosity, Fina stayed back with Ruby in order to let the rest of the party push forward into the unknown. As they gingerly stepped over the door on the floor and entered, Fina noticed nothing had been moved since her search of the room yesterday. The only major difference, of course, was that Granville was tucked away in bed. His arms lay akimbo and his head turned to the side. He wore a pair of jade green silk pyjamas. Fina's observant eyes immediately noticed a brandy glass on the nightstand and an overturned cup and saucer by the bedside.

The Earl approached Granville, peering at his face. He shook him gently and then withdrew, backing up and nearly stepping on the saucer on the floor. His face had turned the colour of the snow outside, and his jowls began to shake as he shook his head in a disbelieving way.

"He's... he's... he's," the Earl stammered. "Get a doctor. Now!" he yelped. Mary, needing no prompting, dashed out of the room.

Charles approached the bed and felt for a pulse. "He's dead," he said in a firm voice, though his hands quivered.

The only sign of disturbance were strange streaks of what looked like coffee, dried on either side of Granville's mouth. His lips were a yellowish-white colour. Fina could see a line of dried brown liquid spittle on one side of his face. Other than this anomaly, he looked as if he were merely in a deep sleep.

"Call a doctor, Grimston!" ordered the Earl.

Grimston, who had managed to remain calm, said evenly, "I'm afraid no one can enter or exit Pauncefort Hall, sir. The snow is simply too deep. I shall notify the local doctor and police via telephone, however. I sincerely doubt they will be able to access the Hall until the weather changes. I will endeavour to enquire into guest medical training."

"Good God, man. Are you telling me we're cut off? And Granville is dead?" Overwhelmed, the Earl fell back into an armchair. Ruby strode into the bathroom – Fina always marvelled at her self-possession in stressful situations – and returned with a glass of water for the Earl. Fina was already sitting in shock on the chair furthest from the bed. Fina, Ruby, Charles, and the now almost-catatonic Earl were those that remained in the bedroom. Well, and the body, thought Fina, grimly.

Ruby turned to Grimston. "I believe Gayatri is training to become a doctor of some sort. You should ask her to come up right away. I can see that nothing can be done, but it would still be useful." Nodding, Grimston slipped out through the bathroom.

Ruby continued, now in full control of the situation. She said to Charles and Fina, "I was nursemaid to my grandfather for many years before he died. I'll attend to the Earl. He has a bad case of shock," she said as she turned back toward the Earl, who was sitting quietly now, completely immobilized.

Fina nodded absently at her friend. Slowly, it dawned on her that this might be an unnatural death. She could see from Charles' rather greenish face that he'd come to the same realization. Keeping out of earshot of the Earl, and unfortunately, thought Fina, Ruby as well, she whispered to Charles. "What did he die of?"

Pulling his vacant stare away from the corpse, Charles said, "I don't know, but it cannot be anything natural. He was too young and fit. Perhaps some sort of accident? Maybe he choked?"

"On what?" Fina asked, simply.

"Good point," he said, despondently. The question prompted Charles to bend over the corpse with a grimace. Fina could see that Granville's mouth was already slightly open. Gently pressing against the lips to open the mouth further, Charles peered into his mouth. He straightened up abruptly, wiped his hands on his trousers and shook his head at Fina.

Out of the corner of her eye, Fina saw the Earl heave himself out of his chair to his feet. He stood for a moment, swaying. Then, with a weak little moan, he crumpled to the floor.

"Fina and Charles!" said Ruby. "Lord Snittlegarth has fainted. Can you two help me with him?"

They rushed to Ruby's side. By the time they carried the Earl over to the settee, Gayatri and Grimston burst in through the bathroom.

"Ahh!" gasped Gayatri. "What happened? Granville... and the Earl! It's just not possible." Fina slipped over to her to explain the situation, and guided her gently to the bedside. Ruby and Grimston joined them there.

Pulling herself together, Gayatri gingerly began her examination. A moment later, she looked up. "Poison," she said, with her mouth set and brows furrowed.

"What?" exclaimed Fina. "Couldn't he have died of some sort of natural causes? He looks so peaceful."

Gayatri shook her head. She stood, rhythmically moving her index finger up and down her nose, apparently lost in thought.

"Do you see the discoloration around his nostrils – in the same colour as the liquid on his cheek? It has a brown, granular appearance. His lips are also discoloured. All of this adds up to internal trauma. Perhaps it was caused by some sort of acid. Rigor has already set in, so I'd say he died sometime last night. Perhaps midnight or near that time? Difficult to determine," said Gayatri.

Shifting on her feet, she continued, "I suppose it could be some sort of unintentional poisoning."

Fina shook her head in bewilderment. In response, Gayatri said, "By that I mean it could have been from food poisoning, though I don't know of any type of food poisoning that would cause this type of visible trauma."

"Well, then that leaves only one possibility," said Ruby, sitting down gently on a nearby chair to steady herself.

"Murder!" they heard from behind them. The three women spun around to see that the Earl was sitting up, shaking his fist, while his jowls flapped furiously. "Granville's been murdered! I knew this day would come."

Amazed by his revival and apparently fantastic oratory skills, Fina said, "What do you mean?"

"I'm sorry," the Earl sputtered. "I should explain. I–I–I had a premonition. No, I'm not superstitious, but I have had a recurring dream about him dying. In my dream, he is suddenly absent. No one at Pauncefort is able to account for his absence – even when I query about his whereabouts. I conclude that something awful – death – has come to him. Though I don't know why I think he actually dies – in the dream, naturally."

"And you never shared this with anyone, Lord Snittlegarth?" asked Gayatri, her eyes narrowing with a pointed gaze.

"Good lord, no," said the Earl. He hesitated. "Except, on one occasion... yes, I did tell Alma, Edgar and Charlotte one time – in passing – at the breakfast table. Granville wasn't with us on that particular weekend. I wouldn't have said it if he had been there. They didn't think much of it at the time, and neither did I. Business affairs were rather weighing on my mind just then, so we all thought it was that, rather than any sort of premonition."

"Please accept our condolences, Lord Snittlegarth," said Gayatri, who made a sudden movement to the bed to cover Granville's face with the sheet, now newly aware of the gravity of the situation, thought Fina. Leaning over stiffly, she scooped up the cup and saucer and put them on the nightstand.

"Should you touch that? Won't the police want everything just so?" asked Fina.

Gayatri stared at her hands as if they weren't her own. "Yes, you're quite right – it was an involuntary reaction. I wonder if the police will be able to reach Pauncefort in this snow before we're forced to move the body."

As no one could answer that question, Ruby padded over to the nightstand, leaned over and stuck her nose into the empty brandy snifter. When she came up for air, she said, "Nothing, no noticeable odour other than brandy. Of course the brandy could mask the odour of a poison." She went down again, this time peering and sniffing at the delicate white cup, decorated with ornate blue patterns – the one that had held the cocoa. "Similar problem," she said.

"I'd leave that for the police if I were you, my girl!" said the Earl sharply. "We may be cut off for the moment, but I've no doubt the authorities will arrive as soon as it's humanly possible to examine the, er, evidence." He spoke the word with distaste.

Fina rolled her eyes, inwardly, at the 'my girl' phrase.

Looking over at Ruby's tight lips, she could see the same thought process playing out in her head as well.

"There may be fingerprints," continued the Earl, a little wildly. "Fingerprints that will allow us to identify the intruder – for an intruder must certainly be the culprit, no doubt whatsoever."

Charles coughed. "The Countess, sir, should be informed. And the other guests."

"What? Oh yes. Charles, look after it, will you?"

As he slipped out of the room, Ruby turned to the Earl. "You spoke of evidence, sir, and the importance of keeping it safe. Quite right. I propose that we keep the cup and snifter some-where secure, perhaps in the jewel safe."

"Yes, yes, quite..." The Earl was fading again, his attention distracted by the supine figure on the bed.

Ruby turned to Fina and whispered, "We need to get to the bottom of this. Let's move quickly. Would you come with me to the kitchen?"

Fina let out a puff of air that lifted her auburn fringe. The fact that this could be murder was only now beginning to dawn on her. Images of her father and brother flashed before her. The trial. The judge. Watching the judge put on the black cap of death. Curse her photographic memory.

Ruby put her hand to Fina's forehead. "Are you all right? I know this is shocking, but I know you're made of sterner stuff. You look like you've seen a ghost."

"I most certainly have," Fina replied, tersely.

Ruby's eyes widened and she gripped Fina's arm. "Oh, I'm so sorry. Of course I should have remembered your family. Will you forgive me? I'm not thinking clearly right now," she said quietly.

Fina's eyes softened and her shoulders relaxed. "I know you didn't mean any harm. Memories, you know. Let's get on with it. I'll be fine."

Wrapping her hand in the sky-blue handkerchief she always carried – one made by her grandmother in St Kitts – Ruby placed the snifter and teacup on a tray stationed on a nearby table and picked it up, balancing it carefully between both hands.

As they made their way downstairs, they heard shouting from the dining room.

15

Peering in, Ruby and Fina confronted a dramatic tableau, reminding Fina of da Vinci's *Last Supper*. The detritus of breakfast was scattered everywhere, but the sweet, comforting aroma they had so enjoyed earlier had vanished. Guests and family were in various states of disarray – heads down, standing up, pacing – all giving the sense that the room was a living organism, even in the face of death. Charles was nowhere to be seen, but clearly he had apprised them of the situation.

Charlotte's face, red and tearstained, glanced up at the newcomers, apparently startled by their presence. She wore a high-necked forest green dress. Rather than flattering her face, Fina noticed it made her body look disconnected from her head, creating a rather spectral effect.

Leslie paced in front of the window, inhaling deeply on a cigarette and muttering to himself. The Countess and Edgar had been bellowing at one another, though Fina hadn't heard what was said. The remainder of the guests sat dejectedly, fidgeting with their silverware.

The Countess peered at Ruby and Fina as if she stumbled

through pea-soup fog. "I gather that you have heard about the... tragedy, my dears."

Both clearly at a loss for words, Fina and Ruby nodded in unison. They slid into chairs near the door though they did not move their legs under the table – ready for a hasty exit.

"Henry must be told, of course... his health... if I posted him a letter today, it might get there by... ah, but I'm forgetting this cursed snow!" cried the Countess. Caught up in her troubles, she seemed hardly to notice that she was speaking her thoughts out loud.

To Fina's right, Cyril topped up what must have been his tenth cup of tea, judging by the way his hands were shaking. Or was there another reason for his heightened state of nerves?

"I know it's not the time, but may I ask why you are taking on serving duties?" Cyril asked Ruby, motioning toward the tray with his teacup.

"We've been asked to put away Granville's glassware, in case they bear traces of unknown chemicals – just as a precaution since the police aren't here."

"Really? Why you two?" queried Cyril imperiously over his wire-rimmed spectacles.

Snapping out of his rhythmic pacing by the window, Leslie spun around. "Yes, dash it, what makes you qualified? And why should we trust you?"

Julia rose to their defence. "I understand that Ruby has some experience with investigation. Besides, there's no way for the police to take them. In case you hadn't noticed it, we're trapped because of the damn snow. And we need to know."

"Know what?" asked Ian.

"If it's poison, you idiot," said Leslie, his eyes flashing. "God, there's so many foreigners in this house – it's probably one of you," he said, waving his finger around the room, at no one in particular, "that did him in."

The Countess leapt to her feet, double chin and formidable bosom shaking. "Mr Dashwood, I know you are a guest here – and we're all upset – but will you kindly leave us alone if you cannot behave. I will not have my other guests insulted."

The left side of Leslie's mouth curled upward. "*Gladly*, Lady Snittlegarth," he snarled sarcastically. He stamped out of the room. The expression 'as bad-tempered as a bag of weasels' drifted through Fina's mind.

"I say good riddance," said Julia with finality.

"Hear, hear, darling," responded Ian.

The argument offered an opening for escape, so Ruby and Fina quietly excused themselves to make their way to the kitchen. Ruby leaned down to whisper into Julia's ear on the way out of the dining room.

As they were descending the stone staircase to the kitchen, Fina asked Ruby, "What did you whisper to Julia?"

"I wanted to see if she still planned to go ahead with our meeting to discuss her wardrobe. She said she didn't see any reason we shouldn't move forward."

"When are we meeting her?"

"In two hours. That gives us plenty of time to see what we can do in the kitchen."

Mrs Lynn was whipping up some concoction with such strength Fina could hear her wheeze from the effort. At the sink behind her, a kitchen-maid scoured a cast-iron pot with considerably less relish. In the meagre daylight, the kitchen's atmosphere was much warmer. The cheerful fire in the hearth also contributed to the cosy domestic scene. She caught a whiff of the smell of warm bread, cooling on a rack in the corner.

Mixing complete, Mrs Lynn turned around and promptly dropped the bowl on the floor. "My dears, you startled me!" she said, in a not-unkind voice.

Fina rushed over to retrieve the bowl with white peaks of

meringue which had fortunately remained unmoved by the tumble. "I've not been myself this morning; not after what happened to Master Granville," Mrs Lynn said, nodding thanks to Fina as she placed the bowl on the counter. "Mary, leave that now," she said over her shoulder to the kitchen-maid. "You want to get those potatoes scrubbed and ready. Look sharp!" The girl scurried off.

"That's why we're here, Mrs Lynn. We don't want to be underfoot, but we need to lock away the glassware Granville used last night. The police will want to know whether there is anything... ah... odd in the dried liquid," said Ruby, motioning to her tray.

"There was nothing wrong with my cocoa, you know!" retorted the cook, hands on hips. "That Mr Clavering and Miss Aston had it too and there was nothing wrong with them, was there? Must have been some sort of other – what do you call it? A natural cause."

"No, no, Mrs Lynn. We are not suggesting there was anything wrong with your cooking. Quite the contrary – your dishes are divine."

Pacified, Mrs Lynn dug in the pocket of her apron. "Very well, miss, I'll unlock the safe for you. Grimston don't mind me having the key – it saves him from having to do all the work himself." She ambled off toward the butler's room.

Ruby whispered, "I'll have a nose around after I've locked up the cups. Would you see what you can learn from the cook while I'm busy? Maybe anything she knows about the family or guests?"

"I'll do my best. I have the impression she has been with the family for a long time. She must know their secrets – I'll see if I can get the gossip flowing," said Fina, looking forward to the challenge.

Once the tray was safely deposited, the cook carefully

dropped the key back into her pocket and patted her apron, as if to tuck the key up for the night. As she turned to the door of the scullery, Fina asked, "Have you been with the family a long time, Mrs Lynn?"

The cook's already thin figure seemed to deflate further. She felt around for a stool as if she had been blinded. Plopping down with a heavy sigh, she said, "I'm sorry, Miss Fina. It's just that what happened to Granville came over me, finally."

Mrs Lynn hugged herself and stared at the fireplace. "You see, I came to Pauncefort Hall well-nigh over twenty years ago, maybe a few years before Granville was born. The Hall was a happy place then – not that it hasn't been since then, mind you – but there was something different about it. I think it was the happiness of Lord and Lady Malvern. Aye, they were a grand couple and thrilled about starting a family. First came Granville, then Charlotte, and then Edgar. The Earl and Countess of Snittlegarth lived in London in those days, but they came to Pauncefort often. Then everything went terribly wrong, Miss Fina."

Mrs Lynn paused, sighed and scratched her hand, meditatively.

Not wanting to lose the momentum of the story, Fina said, "Whatever went wrong, Mrs Lynn?"

"Ah, now, you see, Lady Malvern died suddenly one weekend, when the whole family was having a grand time at the Hall. You see..." She paused in her story to dab her eyes with the corner of her apron. "This horrible death brings back these memories. Lady Malvern died from ptomaine poisoning after a summer picnic. At least, that's what the doctor said at the time. No one questioned it. It was odd, though, because other family members ate some of the cherries as well. We all just assumed that only some of the cherries had spoilt. What was curious, though, was..."

Edgar strode into the room, oddly confident in his gait. Blast it, thought Fina. Just as Mrs Lynn was getting going.

"Mrs Lynn, could you make me some eggs? I'm famished and I missed breakfast," enquired Edgar.

He jumped as he turned his head to see Fina in a nook by the doorway.

"I, I know this must look dashed unfeeling on my part, but I think I'm craving comfort right now," he said.

"Now, sir, you know you have to keep your strength up. I'll hop to it," said the cook, turning toward the stove.

At the sound of another voice, Ruby emerged from the butler's room. "I've heard shock can do that to someone, Edgar," she said. "I expect that's what it is. Please don't let us stop you from taking care of yourself."

"Mmm... very understanding of you, Miss Dove. I appreciate it," he said as he sat at the table with them, running his fingers through his unwashed sandy hair. "I just cannot understand what happened. Julia mentioned that you knew a little about investigating crime. Have you turned anything up so far?"

Ruby looked wary. "I'd have to wait for the official test, but I'm afraid that there is nothing in the snifter or the teacup – or saucer, by the way – that indicates the presence of any sort of toxin. Besides alcohol, of course," she said with a wan smile.

"Nothing at all? Well, that's excellent news!" Edgar said, slapping his hand against the table so hard that a stray teacup toppled over on its side. Fina's stomach lurched as she saw a spray of skin flakes from his fingers fall gently on the cutting board.

"Sorry," he said. Fina was unsure if he were sorry for the exclamation or for tipping over the snifter. "Must have been a medical condition, I suppose."

"Not necessarily, Edgar," said Ruby in a firm voice. "It could be that he simply ingested it elsewhere. No, I tend to agree with Gayatri that this was not a natural death."

"But what else was in the room that he could have eaten?" asked Fina. "Don't poisons act quickly – it must have been something in his room?"

Ruby paused and rubbed her nose. Fina held her breath because she knew this meant that Ruby was about to tell a lie. Perhaps lie was too strong a word. Maybe 'untruth' or 'omission' would be better descriptors. Fina and Ruby had learned each other's 'tell' gestures long ago, for their own protection. Fina felt her cheeks get hot – not because she felt guilty, but because she felt guilty that she knew Ruby was about to tell a lie.

"Actually, there are poisons that may have a delayed effect of this type. I expect that is what happened. I am unfamiliar with these poisons, but I know they exist," she said.

"Well, then it could have been anything!" exclaimed Edgar with exasperation.

"No... not anything. We all ate the same dinner, correct?" Ruby looked toward the cook, who nodded her assent. "And then the men all drank from the same decanters. We'll need to check to see if Granville drank something special – do you know, Edgar?"

Sitting down to a hot plate of eggs, bacon and toast, Edgar answered in between gulps of food.

"He drank brandy like the rest of us. Though at some point I think Granville switched to Scotch and soda. I suppose someone m–m–might have tampered with his glass, though. I'll have to think about it," he said, though he seemed lost in other thoughts as he chomped down on a piece of toast. "Mrs Lynn, these eggs are delicious!"

"I know just how you like them, sir. Always have since you were a little boy," she said.

16

"Let's find somewhere private to talk. My head is positively swimming," suggested Ruby, pointing toward the library door as they ascended the stairs from the kitchen.

Fina felt a soft tickle around her ankle. She looked down to see a little tuxedo cat, tail curved around her feet. A soft plaintive mew and a misty look in the cat's eyes made them irresistible. She bent down and began to coo, scratching the cream-collared shirtfront of the cat.

Ruby leaned back from the library door. "Looks like you've made a friend for life, Feens," she said, bending down to stroke the kitten. Fina knew Ruby was fond of cats, but not in the same way she herself was positively enamoured by them.

"I wonder where the kitten came from – I didn't see her last night," said Fina, straightening up. "Definitely gives us some much-needed comfort after all that's happened."

Ruby nodded as they both sat down in overstuffed chairs in front of the warm glow of the fire. Fina found it difficult to wrap her mind around the fact that they all had sat, chatting in this room, just a few hours before.

"Arggg! Cat!" screeched Fina. The tuxedo kitten had sprung

onto her lap – claws first, of course, as if it were a mountain climber. "Well, I guess you can stay since you've already come," she said in a soft voice, smoothing the fur over, rhythmically.

"Feens, I'm not sure where to begin," said Ruby, rubbing her temples.

"How about we start with your lie?"

"Lie?"

"Yes, why did you lie about the poison?" said Fina, trying to take the sting out of the words by softening her voice.

Ruby stared at her in disbelief, and then Fina saw a flash in her eyes. "I completely forgot that we knew each other's tells," she said, now smiling. "I'll tell you why and then let's back up and review what has happened so far." Fina murmured agreement. "I didn't want to tell anyone at the time – just because they might get the wrong idea – but I do know what poison killed Granville."

Fina's hand stopped in the middle of the kitten's back and stayed there. She just sat motionless, waiting for Ruby to continue.

"I know the effects of the concentrated oxalic acid stain remover I used on Gayatri's dress last night. Though oxalic acid can be found from a number of common plant sources, this particular concentrate is derived from my grandmother's garden in St Kitts. It has been used in my family for generations. My grandmother first taught me how to identify it, dry the leaves and then pulverize them into a fine powder. You add a little water to make it into a paste to put on a textile to remove the stain. It takes many uses to make it work, though, so I developed a concentrate at the lab in Oxford."

"And you think it's what caused his death?"

"The main point is that it is terrifically poisonous, as I said last night. My grandmother once told me a story about someone who had been enslaved on the island and had exacted revenge on the master. The results of the poison were exactly the same as those we saw on Granville's body. I remember them well because they're so distinctive – and my grandmother was a very vivid storyteller."

"How long does it take for the poison to take effect?" asked Fina, now cradling the kitten for her own comfort as much as that of the cat's.

"Maybe fifteen to twenty minutes, no more than that. Of course, the dosage might make it happen a bit more quickly, but it would have to be fairly substantial," she replied. "Normal oxalic acid poisoning actually takes days. But not my concentrate."

"So that means it must have been just before he went upstairs to bed, or just after when he was in bed."

"Yes, although I couldn't smell any oxalic acid in either the snifter or the cup, and it's pretty whiffy stuff. I should clarify – pure oxalic acid is odourless, but my stain remover concoction is not."

"Hmm," said Fina. "Is it possible that he could have drunk the lot, leaving no trace?"

Ruby shrugged. "I suppose so. But it's unlikely. There was a tiny amount of dried liquid in the bottom of both the snifter and the cup."

The cat curled into a ball on Fina's lap, covering its face with its tiny paw, oblivious to the seriousness of their discussion. Fina wished she could join along in the blissful release. She gazed out the window: the snow was still falling lightly.

"Feens – are you there?" asked Ruby, not unkindly.

Fina shivered. "Yes. Sorry. I'm having trouble focusing... So what you're suggesting, to be clear, is that the poison must have been ingested before he went to bed – perhaps from another glass? There's no way the killer could have switched the teacup or the snifter because the doors were bolted from the inside."

Leaning forward in a stretch, Ruby said, "Yes. Do you mind if we go through the evening, step by step, to figure out what happened?"

Before they could begin, Fina's head snapped up at the sound of a soft footfall behind her. She gave Ruby a warning gesture. Had someone been there all the time? How much had they overheard?

The footsteps came closer. They sounded strangely menacing. Fina, holding her breath, felt sure that whoever was with them in the library had come in with evil intentions. Her fingernails gripped the plush velvet upholstery.

A sudden gasp made them both jump. "Blimey!" said Charles, peering around the edge of the high-back wing chair that had hidden the women from his sight. "You gave me a fright!"

Fina collapsed into the cushions. "You gave us a worse one!" She noticed the kitten, unperturbed, had peeled back one eye to see who had the audacity to interrupt her slumber.

"I came to stoke the fire," he said, pushing the charred logs with a poker, sending up sparks as one fell on another. "The house is in a state. Grimston has just announced that the telephone line is out of order, thanks to the snow. The Earl is ranting and raving, Lady Charlotte is crying, the Countess is in a true state of blank-faced shock, and the guests are all behaving in a very anxious manner. I'm anxious myself," he said. His hand closed over his mouth. "Begging your pardon, ladies. I forgot myself in your company. I shouldn't be discussing the guests and the family in this way. I forget myself around you, for some reason," he said, quickly glancing at Fina and then looking away hastily.

"I expect it's because the three of us don't move in such aristocratic circles," said Ruby.

Charles nodded and bent down to stroke the cat, after securing permission to do so from Fina with a smile.

"This here's little Grayling," he said, affectionately. "She must have been separated from her mother – she's clearly the runt of the litter. The little cheeky layabout wandered to the back door of the kitchen about a month ago. She hopped up on the counter when Mrs Lynn wasn't looking and made away with the fish on the counter."

"Hence the name Grayling," said Fina, grinning. "My brother used to fish," she said, her voice catching on the last syllable. Fond and painful memories flashed momentarily – again.

Redirecting the conversation quickly, Ruby asked, "So what do you think happened, Charles?"

Straightening up, he pulled over a short stool to sit in front of the fire. Scratching his head, he said, "I don't have any particular theories – mostly because Granville was disliked by so many people at Pauncefort this weekend. But I cannot see any of them hating him enough to commit murder. Mind you, it was a timid sort of crime – if you can ever say that about murder."

"I hadn't thought of it that way," said Fina. "You mean because it was some sort of poison?"

Fina did not want to give away the fact that they suspected Ruby was the source of the poison. She saw her friend's fists relax themselves from their clenched position.

Charles nodded and stared at Grayling. "Mind you, there are some people who were more or less indifferent to him, but that doesn't mean they don't have a grudge I don't know about. His family loved him, but didn't particularly like him – if you know what I mean. I suppose Leslie was the only one who seemed to be fond of him."

"Perhaps before we get to reasons for his death, we should recount what happened, so we can eliminate some people from the list of possible suspects," said Ruby. Though Ruby most definitely had her playful side, Fina knew that pressure brought out her need for orderly behaviour and contemplation.

Ruby continued, "Fina and I were just diving into this subject when you arrived. Though I couldn't find any trace of poison in the glassware in his room, Granville had to have ingested something – most likely before he went to bed. Unless he had some chocolates or some other late-night snack hidden in his room, the poison had to be in something he drank before going to bed."

"Yes, because he must have gone to bed after he had that argument with Edgar in the study," said Fina.

"What argument?" interjected Charles. "How do you know the two of them had an argument?" He spoke casually, but there was a hint of suspicion in his voice, Fina noted.

Ruby rose from her seat and began to pace around the room. Nervous energy, thought Fina. *Now I've gone and put my foot in it.*

"Ahem," said Fina. "What I mean is, well, we thought... we just happened to..."

"Happened to what?" said Charles, voice still even – but strangely flat, thought Fina.

"What Fina means is that we were eavesdropping," said Ruby.

Charles grinned. "Rather cheeky of you. What were you doing up? I thought you'd gone to bed."

"We were rather famished, so we went downstairs to get a bite to eat," said Ruby. "We heard this row in the study – before Mrs Lynn provided us with some provisions in the kitchen."

"I see," said Charles. His voice had changed, so Fina thought he found the story to be plausible. Was it relief she could hear in his tone? He ploughed on. "What was the row about?"

Fina said, "Granville told Edgar he wouldn't fund the named professorship for Professor Lighton. He also said, 'I know what you did' – which must have something to do with the college?" she said, looking enquiringly at Ruby.

"Perhaps," said Ruby, noncommittally.

Fina wondered about Ruby's tepid response. Then she realized that 'I know what you did' could refer to the massacre at Bluegate – something they couldn't reveal to Charles because it would disclose the true reason for their weekend at Pauncefort. If it did, that would mean Edgar had known about what happened in St Kitts. And he might not be minded to keep it secret, either. Fina's mind flew back to what Gayatri had said in the library the previous night. She had been very vague about whether Edgar was the one who had asked her down for the weekend. Could he have been the one who arranged for the sisters to receive the Bluegate papers?

Sitting down again in the chair near the fire, Ruby said, "Now we need to rely on Fina's fabulous photographic memory. Do you remember if they still had their drinks when they came out of the study?"

Fina wrenched her mind back to the here and now. "I don't remember whether Edgar had a glass in his hand, but I do remember that Granville did. It looked to be the same as the one in the bedroom this morning, but that doesn't mean anything in particular," she said. Surely they'd heard the noise of Edgar's glass being slammed down on the table, just before he'd left.

Charles frowned. "So does that mean that the only person who could have poisoned Granville was his brother – since they were the last ones in the study?"

"It's true, he was acting rather cavalier this morning," said Fina thoughtfully. "Wasn't he, Ruby?"

"Tucking into eggs and bacon, you mean?" Ruby said with a smile. "Hardly the mark of a murderer! Also, you're forgetting that Edgar appeared to have the upper hand over Granville when they parted last night. He wouldn't have resorted to such drastic measures if he was able to influence him another way."

"Selkies and kelpies," sighed Fina, "this is getting complicated."

Charles broke in, "Selkies and kelpies? Aren't they Scottish folklore?"

"Hmph. Yes, they are. But my uncle was Scottish. It was an expression he used," retorted Fina, feeling strangely defensive. "And besides, there are selkies in Irish folklore, too."

"Ah, I see. Sorry for derailing our train of thought," said Charles, looking at Ruby, who had returned to pacing by the window.

"In any case, we're assuming the snifter held the poison. What about the teacup that held the cocoa?" asked Ruby. "That might open up some more possibilities."

Turning toward Charles, Fina asked, "Would you ask the cook about the cocoa? Perhaps she noticed something out of the ordinary with it. I wonder whether she actually saw Ian and Julia make their own cocoa. And maybe talk to other staff who might have seen something?"

How lucky they were to have someone on the staff they could trust, she thought. Charles was so steadfast; you only had to look at him to see he was an honest man. Without him, they would have had to work so much harder to find out what had happened.

"I'd be happy to talk to Mrs Lynn – we get on well," said Charles smoothly. "I assume you two will talk to the guests and the family and see what you can find out. Let's try to meet up again to chat. Perhaps this afternoon?"

In a state of nervous anticipation, they floated aimlessly from the library. Grayling remained, curled up in front of the hearth. Fina wished she could curl up and forget this nightmare as well.

17

"It's disappeared!" exclaimed Ruby, as she overturned her travelling bag and shook it as if her life depended on it. Perhaps it did, thought Fina.

Perched on the edge of the bed – the only place in Ruby's bedroom not covered in some item of clothing by now – Fina pawed at the air to calm down her friend. It was odd to see her in such a frenzied state. She had never seen anything so unnerve Ruby.

"What does it look like? Don't worry, we'll find it," said Fina.

Ruby's voice quivered, "It's a small glass bottle – the size of a bottle for headache tablets or tooth powder. I could have sworn that I left it on the top of my dressing table after helping Gayatri with her dress. It is emerald green with a cut-glass stopper. A cross between a decanter and a perfume bottle, I suppose. It's exquisite, really. Though I couldn't care less right now if it were in a dirty tin box or not. We need to find it!"

In her uncharacteristic fury, Ruby continued to throw clothes around the room as if she were throwing salt over one shoulder with superstitious abandon.

"Ruby..." said Fina.

Ruby straightened up, smoothed her hair and regained her composure. "You're right, Feens. No way to go about it."

"Actually, I was going to suggest that the most likely explanation is that the murderer stole the bottle. You never lose anything. *I'm* the one who loses everything! Remember when I lost the first draft of your term paper?"

Ruby scowled at the memory and then smiled. "Yes, you're right. I still don't forgive you for that," she said, tossing a yellow scarf at Fina that fell lightly on her nose. "My mother always tried to be positive in these situations. I'm going to try to follow her sage advice, for once." But the light mood didn't last. "This, though, is much more serious. If we don't stay calm and use our heads, things could look rather grim for us."

Fina had no answer. Her mind was ensnared in a web of painful memories. She heard once again the heavy-handed knock at the door, the denial and shock she had felt at her brother's arrest.

Clearing her throat, Ruby continued, "So let's assume the murderer stole my stain remover. The upside to this news is that this confirms it must be the poison, correct?"

Fina nodded. "Which means we can fix the time Granville took it as fifteen to twenty minutes – maximum – before he climbed into bed."

"That means the poison can't have been in the brandy snifter. Unless—" Ruby stopped short.

"Yes?"

"Unless someone dropped it in before Granville reached his room. We weren't the only ones up and about last night, remember?"

"So we weren't," said Fina thoughtfully. She recalled Edgar's rage in the library, and the furtive way Cyril had scurried up the stairs. Hadn't that been a brandy glass he was carrying?

Ruby had already moved on. "Then there's the cocoa. It

would have been hot, so he would want to drink it as soon as possible, perhaps sitting up in bed. If the cocoa was poisoned, we can fix the approximate time of death close to whenever the cook brought it up. We'll find that out from Charles soon," she said, no longer distracted by the loss of the bottle and the clothing tempest of her room.

Sitting down and apparently following her own train of thought, Ruby continued. "Let's set the scene. Granville stumbles into his bedroom, drunk and possibly upset."

"Holding a brandy snifter that is not yet empty," interjected Fina.

"Yes, though it is possible that there was already a glass in his bedroom – from earlier in the day or evening – or even from the day before."

"I think that's unlikely, since I didn't see one in his room when I searched earlier," said Fina.

"I forgot about that! Yes. So, he enters the room with the brandy, pulls the bell for cocoa. Then he could have just sat there until the cocoa came, though the more likely scenario is that he prepared for bed."

Pushing aside a pile of clothes threatening to topple over on her, Fina said, "Let's assume he's in his pyjamas, waiting for the cocoa. The cocoa arrives, he takes it, gets into bed and then drinks it while reading. Perhaps he's already finished off his brandy."

"Or maybe he puts it in his cocoa for a midnight treat," said Ruby. "In any case, he could have finished the brandy after the cocoa or vice versa, so it doesn't get us any closer to identifying what was the source of the poison," she sighed.

"But at least we've established more or less how it was done," said Fina with growing enthusiasm. "Now we just need to work out why. No shortage of motives, unfortunately. I suppose we'll know more after luncheon and our wardrobe interview with Julia."

Ruby glanced at the mantelpiece clock, covered in a stray stocking. She removed the stocking and lovingly folded it into a drawer. Looking back at the now-naked clock, she said, "Heavens, it's 12:50! We'll be late to Julia's! I'll tidy this later... and find that bloody poison."

As they entered the hallway, Fina grasped Ruby's arm. "What happens if the police arrive?"

"Well, as we're apparently experiencing the blizzard of the century, I don't think they'll be making their appearance too readily," said Ruby.

"What I meant was, what do we do when they *eventually* arrive? They will, sooner or later. I'm trying to take this all one step at a time, but it is hard. This is my first mission. I had all sorts of images in my head of someone lurking behind a large chair and then leaping out and saying 'gotcha' or some such Americanism, or even worse, failing you and myself," said Fina looking furtively up and down the hall.

Ruby shoved her hands in her dress pockets and sighed. "I know, I know. I've been thinking the same, over and over. There are three points we should not lose sight of. First, we cannot let anyone know about our 'mission', as you say—"

"Should we hide the Bluegate papers somewhere?" said Fina. "Sorry – I didn't mean to interrupt."

"No, no, it's all right. I've taken care of it."

Fina nodded. Perhaps Ruby had already handed the papers over to Gayatri or Sajida. She felt a bit miffed that she hadn't spotted the secret sign, the one which signalled that the sisters were the point of contact. But discretion was the better part of valour, after all.

"The second point," Ruby continued, "is that we really must find out who murdered Granville, because when the police come, suspicion will definitely point in my direction when they find out it was my stain remover."

"Yes, but everyone knew you had the poison, so anyone could have taken it from you. Remember when you made the announcement about Gayatri's dress during cocktails? Everyone was present and paying attention. Besides, you no longer have the poison," said Fina, triumphantly.

Ruby shook her head, ruefully. "If there's one thing we both know from our personal experiences with the police – you for a very specific reason, and me because of an ironically general reason – we know they'll see me as the culprit."

"I know you're right, you're right," Fina said, balling up her fist. "What's the third point?"

"It's related to the second. If we find out who did it – and we must – then we have two options. We tell the police – which I know we both completely disagree with given what we know about prison and hanging..."

"Or?" asked Fina. "What's the alternative?"

"We have to concoct a way the murderer is held responsible but that also lets the case go cold – from the viewpoint of the police," Ruby said, letting out a gush of air. "And I have no idea how we're going to do that. But we must..."

Slam. Footsteps approached around the corner. They involuntarily flattened themselves against the wall, as if they were schoolgirls loitering in the hall and the headmistress was approaching.

Sajida rounded the corner, head down, lost in thought. Looking up, she grabbed her chest. She let out a tiny gasp. "I'm sorry I didn't see you there. I suppose we're all on edge."

Peering closer at Sajida, Fina noticed circles around her eyes, as if she had taken a pencil to them. Her natural ebullience had subsided. Her shoulders hunched which had the effect of making her appear almost the same height as Fina.

"Have you seen my sister? I can't find her anywhere. She came down from the – ah – scene of the crime, I suppose, after breakfast. She said she had something to attend to but I haven't seen her since," Sajida said, clutching at her gorgeous cream-coloured skirt with a fist.

Ruby reached out and gently stroked her upper arm, as if to both calm her and warm her up. "I'm sure she's about. Paunce-fort is a grand, spacious hall, after all. Have you checked with Grimston or Charles? Perhaps they know. I'm not sure where Grimston might be, but I believe Charles should be in the kitchen – or at least returning from the kitchen."

She pursed her lips. "I haven't and I'll try that." She scuttled off down the dimly lit corridor.

When they arrived at last at Julia's bedroom – after a few unintentional detours – they found the door wide open. Jazz floated out softly. After knocking lightly and poking her head around the door frame, Fina saw Julia and Gayatri's heads bent together in intense conversation. Fina could not make out whether it was a discussion or quarrel.

"Lovely music, Julia," said Ruby as she slipped in next to Fina. "Did you bring your own gramophone?"

Bouncing up to greet them, Julia said, "I travel with it everywhere. Sometimes you have to be the life of the party yourself – and to have a party by oneself, for that matter. These weekends can become rather dreary," she stopped herself mid-sentence as if her air source had been cut off. "I expect listening to music right now seems insensitive or gauche."

Fina sensed the statement was a challenge rather than an apology.

Playing along, Ruby responded, "Absolutely not. I always say one has to keep a positive outlook, especially when the world looks bleak." Satisfied that this was the close to the conversation,

Julia sidled up to Ruby and demanded to know her opinion on the latest Paris designs of trousers.

Gayatri smiled in the corner, but did not participate in the conversation. She sipped her tea in a casual manner. Fina thought there was something studied about her casualness – as if she knew she were being watched.

Fina approached her and smiled, not wanting to worry her. "Your sister is anxious – she didn't know where you were. I sent her toward the kitchen to find you," said Fina.

"Oh, oh – thank you," she said, nearly dropping her teacup in her haste to leave the room.

"What was that all about?" asked Julia, barely looking up from Ruby's sketchbook.

"Gayatri went to find her sister – they've been missing each other all morning." Why did Fina feel like she was making an excuse for them? Certainly the morning had been stressful for them all, but wasn't this a bit of an overreaction to the murder? It's not as if either sister had been terribly close to Granville. In fact they'd seemed to be at pains to stay out of his way.

"Mmm..." said Julia, noncommittally. Ruby gave Fina encouragement with a slight upturn of her chin.

Taking the cue, Fina swished her skirts casually and plopped down next to Julia on the settee. "What do you think, Julia? Have any theories about what happened?"

Julia squinted for a split second, but then straightened her back and leaned her head against the wall. She stared vacantly at a rather insipid landscape of what might have been the local village hanging on the opposite wall. "Well, Leslie Dashwood is pretty ghastly – if you ask me. A perfect bore. He seemed to be one of the few people on this earth that genuinely appreciated Granville, though."

She took a long drag on her cigarette before continuing her dossier. "That Lighton character has shifty eyes, but I suspect it has something to do with his political beliefs," she said, winking at Fina. "Gayatri and Sajida know – I mean knew – Granville, but I cannot see them having any obvious need to do him in. Then there's the family. I had heard that Granville threatened to turn out his aunt and uncle once his father died – I understand Lord Malvern is not long for this vale of tears."

"What do you mean – turn them out of Pauncefort?" asked Ruby.

"Yes, that's it. I cannot remember where I heard that from – perhaps Charlotte? I know that he's made a similar threat against Charlotte and Edgar. Apparently once the old man pops off everything goes to Granville – with a tiny allowance for the rest of the family. Edgar and Charlotte might get by... though Charlotte would have to marry to keep up her standards. But the aunt and uncle would be in the proverbial soup."

A little breathlessly, Fina dared to continue. "What about Ian? I know you're close – have you spoken about what happened?"

Ruby added, "We're just trying to figure this out since the police cannot be here."

"Quite, quite – I can see wanting to play sleuth. I'd be careful, though. You don't want to end up like those detective novels," said Julia with her mouth curved upwards in one corner – in the same way one lifted one eyebrow, thought Fina.

"No, no, of course," said Fina, spluttering. "There are two of us, though, so we should be safe. Besides, I cannot get that image of the body out of my mind. We have to do something."

Julia stiffened at the word 'body'.

Ruby returned to their enquiry. "So, I find Ian quite charming..."

"I saw that last night at dinner," said Julia, grinning maliciously.

She doesn't mince her words, thought Fina, slightly shocked. But perhaps that was part of what made her so likeable.

Ruby continued on, her unflappable self. "What was his connection to Granville? Is he somehow involved in the sugar business? He told me about his Caribbean connections last night at dinner."

"Oh... I see the cat is out of the bag. I suppose it might have been the reason they first crossed paths. But no, he came here to talk to Granville about investing in a few of his upcoming productions. They're going to be grand dramas – and I hope to be the leading lady in them. I'd love for you to design the costumes, Ruby," she said, shamelessly trying to divert the conversation.

Fina thought she'd push her luck before Julia was successful in derailing their enquiry. She was still outwardly nonchalant, but Fina noticed that she was definitely sitting up straighter now, no longer in her usual languid 'I-don't-have-a-care-in-the-world-darling' pose.

"It's odd that I didn't see Ian last night. Was he with you, perhaps, Julia? Did you have any late-night cocoa?" Fina thought she would see if Julia were ready to lie. She felt a warm glow at her ability to practise deception without turning crimson every time.

Julia's eyes narrowed. She stubbed out her cigarette in the already-brimming ashtray. She extracted an exquisitely engraved silver cigarette case from her blazer, which was slung over the nearest chair. Then she offered it up as if she were pointing out an important passage in a book. Ruby and Fina declined with small shakes of their heads. Julia's graceful ignition procedure with that mother-of-pearl lighter impressed Fina.

Blowing a halo of smoke away from both women, Julia deigned to answer the question. "So many questions... but fair enough. I left for bed perhaps thirty minutes or so after you two left. I was peckish, so I did go down to make myself some cocoa. I was roundly scolded by the cook for not ringing for it. That's it. I suppose you could say that I was irritated by Granville's advances... but that's hardly a reason for killing him."

"Advances?" asked Fina. "Do you mean advances on a contract?"

Julia giggled. "No, no. I mean he was simply potty about me. Didn't you notice how he'd made sheep's eyes at me during dinner?"

Ruby rescued Fina as she felt her face turn scarlet. Damn, there I go again, thought Fina.

"I did notice some admiring glances, now that you mention it. Is that why he wants to fund Ian's productions?" asked Ruby.

"I suppose so. Ian's task this weekend was to convince him that it was a good investment, poor baby. Especially since Granville was to become head of the family business."

So she knew about that. Fina wondered if this was common knowledge among the other guests.

Tap-tap. Ian's head appeared around the door frame.

"Speak of the devil, sweetie!" said Julia, springing up. Hands in his Savile Row grey suit pockets, Ian approached, planting air kisses around Julia. "Talking about me again? I know I'm on the tips of everyone's tongues," he said, smiling roguishly at Ruby. Ruby pretended not to notice, but did smooth back her hair.

He pointed to his watch and said, "Time for luncheon, ladies. I'm famished, so let's get a move on downstairs."

18

Lunch was a simple affair, no doubt due to the grim circumstances, thought Fina. Despite a ravenous appetite, Fina did her best to control her obvious inhalation of the soup. She looked around in panic for a roll. Cyril, the apparent keeper of the rolls, primly distributed one to her with the tongs – as if he were under orders to ration wheat supplies.

Mildly satiated, Fina eased back into her chair. She considered the atmosphere of the dining room. One of the first compliments Ruby had paid her when they first met was to note Fina's uncanny ability to pin down the atmosphere of a room. She supposed one of her more bohemian friends might call it 'energy'. Energy was certainly the right word for this gathering at the moment. No, not energy – electricity. If she reached out to touch the Earl, seated next to her, she was quite sure that the hairs on their arms would stand at attention. The situation was tense, to be sure – one look at the dour countenance of the usually jovial Earl confirmed that – as if they had just survived a stormy voyage. They certainly all looked seasick.

And yet they all talked excitedly to one another. Nibbling on a delicious salmon sandwich, Fina dared to look over at Leslie.

His head was bent, as he chased a small potato in a circle on his plate. Though he sat at the end of the long table, she could see that his eyes were red. Swollen as a frog in the autumn.

From the other end of the table, the Countess bellowed, "My dear guests..."

Startled, Fina dropped her sandwich on her plate, just missing Cyril's lap. Fina could see the Countess looked surprised by the volume of her own voice.

"I know we're all in a state of bereavement, but I thought it important that we continue on with our routines. That is why I asked cook to prepare a light luncheon," the Countess said, sweeping her hand around the table in a rather theatrical manner.

Heads turned as Edgar stumbled into the room. Ruby caught Fina's eye and gave her a look of exasperation. Oh dear, thought Fina. Edgar is dead drunk.

"Yes, dearest Auntie," said Edgar, raising his glass, "Here's to English hospitality and stiff facial muscles... or some such rot." He toasted the table, but most particularly, Fina noticed, in the direction of Leslie. Leslie's eyes remained glued to his potato companion on his plate. Edgar proceeded to gulp the remainder of his beverage of choice. Perhaps brandy. Perhaps whisky. In any event, thought Fina, it was definitely high alcohol content.

Edgar had not finished. "And where were all of you, I ask, when my dearest brother was murdered? Let's hear your protestations of innocence!" he slurred. Though his sentences lacked the usual pauses customary between words, Fina noticed he had lost his stuttering and stammering habit. His clothes were in an appalling state, as if he had taken a nap in them.

Charlotte rose from her seat. With a stealthy crouching movement, she crept toward Edgar, like a tiger closing in on a drunken goat. The Earl motioned to Charlotte to sit down. "Thank you, my dear," he said in a near whisper.

More loudly now, the Earl said, "Yes, Nephew, I think you're right. Let's hear it from everyone. The police are not here, but we may as well get it all straight for them when they do arrive, so that they don't leap to any silly conclusions. So we'd better find out this, this..." he trailed off, at an apparent loss for words. Regaining his footing, he said, curtly, "Though I think you'd better sit down, dear boy."

Grimston materialized from the ether and gently piloted Edgar to the nearest chair. His lids were lowered to a half-mast position, only occasionally jerking open at random intervals.

One problem solved, the Earl fixed his gaze on each guest in a slow, panoptic-like motion around the long oval table. Either by design or chance, thought Fina, the last person subjected to the sharp eye of Lord Snittlegarth was Cyril Lighton.

"Well, dash it. I suppose I had better begin, then," said the professor. Fina noticed he had a fine sheen of sweat forming on his brow and around the edges of his combed moustache. Licking his lips, he began. "I don't know exactly what we're supposed to report, but I went up to bed around say, 11pm. Everyone else had retired – at least that I could see – with the exception of Granville and Edgar. I took my leave of them in the study. I prepared for the night and then read – in bed – for perhaps a quarter of an hour. Promptly fell asleep. Reading Hobbes does that to me. Slept soundly but I did get up once in the middle of the night. Call of nature and all that..." He tapped his fingers on the table. Fina thought it seemed forced – as if he were willing himself to appear casual. "Then I awoke at precisely 9am, as I invariably do. I came down to breakfast shortly thereafter."

Fina noticed Ruby drawing in her diaphragm. "But you have left something out, Professor Lighton," said Ruby, exhaling what seemed to be anticipation and relief. All eyes turned to Ruby and then back to Cyril as if it were the opening of a tennis match.

"What do you mean, Miss Dove?" he blustered, voice rising. "I didn't leave anything out," he said, then hesitating, "And if I did, it was unintentional."

Eyes from around the table rolled back to Ruby. "Fina and I saw you leave the study – and you were clearly not on good terms with Granville," she said, halting her speech, mid-sentence. Fina knew her friend well enough to realize that she herself realized her mistake. Now everyone would ask what they were doing downstairs at that time.

Recovering quickly, Ruby blurted out just as Cyril was opening his mouth, "In case you're wondering, Fina and I were hungry, so we thought we'd have a rummage around in the kitchen."

Cyril's brow furrowed – he clearly felt deprived of the opportunity to seek revenge against Ruby. "Yes, well, Miss Dove, I don't see how that's important. It became a disagreement between two brothers after I left," he said, throwing his napkin on his plate with a final flourish – signalling the interview had ended.

Fina accepted the proverbial baton from Ruby and carried on. "I'm afraid we cannot ask Edgar at the moment," she said, glancing over at the slumped figure at the edge of the table, now snoring gently. "So would you please tell us yourself?"

Though it was already quiet, Fina could feel a deeper hush descend on the room. Cyril removed his glasses. Absently, he began to wipe them with the napkin he had rejected a moment ago. He persisted in this activity long after even the most perfectionist parlourmaid would have pronounced the lenses clean, Fina thought.

"Granville was going to sponsor a named professorship at Oxford. Notions of grandeur, I suppose, and all that. Well, when Granville found out that I was going to be the beneficiary of this position, he, he said he would withdraw all funds immediately," Cyril said, shifting in his chair and pulling at his collar. He stared at Edgar in the corner, as if by sheer force of will he could shake him out of his inebriated state.

"And?" said Leslie, who had managed to pull his attention away from his potato. "Why on earth would he do such a thing?" he queried, in a tone that indicated he already knew the answer to his own question.

"Well... dash it. When Granville discovered my political leanings – to the left that is – he became absolutely opposed to the idea. Granville is a fascist supporter, of course."

"Fascist? Fascist!" roared the Earl. "What do you mean by that, sir? How dare you defame my nephew!" He began to raise himself from the chair.

The Countess tugged at his arm. "Roger, please, I'm sure he didn't mean it."

"On the contrary, Countess. He is a fascist. Or I should say he was a fascist," said Gayatri quietly. Sajida looked at her sister in alarm.

"Precisely my point," said Cyril, looking bolstered by the gathering support. "I'm not using it to defame him, I'm simply describing his political affiliations," he said, perching his immaculate glasses back on his nose.

Aware that this conversation was derailing quickly, Fina intervened. "Professor Lighton, could Granville have actually carried out his threat of withdrawing funds for the named professorship?"

"Yes, though not without the potential to crack open a major scandal. My, ah... political activities would be exposed, and that would look bad for Edgar and perhaps the family as a whole. Hard to say. In any case, Granville didn't seem to mind – at least not at the time. I supposed Edgar and I both believed he would see sense by morning," he said, now in a somewhat shaky tone.

"Hrmph," mumbled the Earl. "Let's hear what the others have to say. You!" he barked, nodding at Leslie.

"I say, Lord S., I was absolutely devoted to Granville. You know that," said Leslie in a hushed tone. While not letting her first impression go, Fina did shift her view of the cad in that moment. He appeared to be genuinely grieving, unlike anyone else at the table.

The Earl himself looked taken aback by the display of emotion. "Ahem, yes, well. Of course, my boy, of course."

"I went up to bed when the party broke up in the saloon," Leslie said in a quavering voice. "Then I went to bed – no cocoa, no midnight meanderings. Just bed. I woke up around 9am this morning and came straight down to breakfast."

"Of course you did, dear," cooed the Countess, clearly upset by Leslie's display of grief.

The Earl, anxious to leave this scene behind, shifted his gaze to Ian. "And you, sir?" clearly having forgotten Ian's name, thought Fina.

"My name is Ian Clavering, sir," said Ian in an evenly controlled voice. "And I followed the same routine as Mr Dashwood. Except I did go down to make myself some cocoa. As for a reason to wish Granville ill, I haven't one," he said, pulling at his earlobe.

Ah, thought Fina, that must be his tell.

"Sweetie, you know that isn't true," said Julia, nudging him playfully. She spread her arms around the table and proclaimed, "I'll explain as I am a part of the possible motive."

While Julia delicately explained the nature of Granville's feelings toward her, Fina saw Charles slip into the room. He gave her a wink and then stood in the corner, gazing at the similarly impassive deer head mounted on the opposite wall.

Returning her gaze back to the uncomfortable gathering,

Fina refocused on the conversation at hand. Gayatri was speaking.

"Sajida and I went upstairs after the music ended in the saloon. We were both quite tired from the journey. We have adjoining rooms. We are both light sleepers, so one of us would have noticed if the other left her room," she said.

"Precisely!" declared Leslie, dropping his fork with a clatter on his plate. "You both put each other in the clear. One of you could be covering for the other, or you could both have been in on it together. And how can we trust your so-called medical skills, anyway?"

"Now, Leslie," said Charlotte, in a low, warning voice. Fina had completely forgotten she was at the table. "We are very grateful to Gayatri for assisting us at all. I'm sure we don't doubt her medical expertise," she said with finality.

"That's all well and good, but I still say the two of them have the perfect opportunity. Besides, they're women," shot back Leslie. "Their alibis are complete and utter tosh."

"Be that as it may," retorted Cyril. "Why in heaven's name would they do such a thing? Either separately, or jointly?"

All eyes turned to Gayatri and Sajida expectantly. Sajida spoke up this time. "We haven't any reason to wish him harm," said Sajida confidently. Fina noticed that Gayatri was holding her breath when her sister spoke. Was it because she was worried she would say something revealing or was it just normal older sister nervousness on behalf of the younger?

"What about you, Charlotte?" asked Sajida, pulling her lips into a smile that almost revealed her gums.

"Good gracious, how can you ask such a question, Miss Badarur? His own sister?" said the Countess. Her Chelsea bun hairstyle quivered and threatened to unleash itself. The Earl covered her hand in a gentle embrace.

"It's quite alright, Auntie," said Charlotte. "Everyone should account for their whereabouts, including the two of you. As for me, my story is much the same as the others – though I did stay behind a few minutes after the party ended in the saloon to check with Grimston about arrangements for the following day. Oh, I did go down to speak to the cook to confer with her about our rations – given the blizzard."

At the mention of snow, everyone looked to the windows. Fina felt an inward collective groan was given at the sight of the falling flakes. Was that hail pelting at the window? It certainly heightened the tension in the room.

"As for a grudge against Granville, I haven't any, nor can I think of anything that could be possibly interpreted that way," said Charlotte, pausing in between the din caused by the hail. Fina noticed her exquisite emerald earrings flickering in the dim light as she shook her head. She bent her head to the side and looked expectantly toward her aunt.

Heaving a rather noticeable sigh, the Countess said, "This is rather tiresome. I am Granville's aunt, after all. As you all know, I retired rather early. A headache was imminent and I also wanted to attend to some correspondence. I didn't leave my room – and fell asleep around 11pm. I awoke this morning at 9:30 and immediately came to breakfast," she said, pushing away her plate. "And if you're asking why I should harm him, well... pish. Stuff and nonsense." She passed the verbal baton by turning her head to her husband.

The Earl grumbled. "So sorry, m'dear." He patted his wife's hand like a small dog. "After the gathering in the saloon, I had a snifter or two with the gentlemen in the study. Then I retired to bed. I'm not sure what time it was, but I suppose it must have been 10:30. I said goodnight to my dear wife," he said, dipping his head toward her, "and woke up around nine this morning. Came straight down to breakfast."

"Ahem." Everyone turned toward the doorway.

"Yes, Grimston?" said the Earl.

Grimston stepped forward, lowered his hand from his mouth and said in a grave tone, "This is highly unorthodox, but I feel it is timely to report on the whereabouts of the servants – as everyone is present."

"Good thinking, Grimston. Have you interviewed the staff?" asked the Earl.

Grimston's body remained stiff, but Fina saw his lips release ever so slightly at the encouragement. "Yes, sir. Charles and I endeavoured to interview all of the staff – even though there are few of us given the inclement weather."

"Well, out with it, man," said the Earl.

Charles stepped forward. "As Grimston was busy with many arrangements, sir, I took the liberty of interviewing the staff. The only person who had any interaction with Master Granville after everyone went to bed was Mrs Lynn, the cook. She told us he rang for cocoa just after 11:30 and she took it up to him herself approximately fifteen minutes later. Mrs Lynn didn't notice anything unusual about him, sir. He was in his nightclothes when he opened the door for the cocoa."

"Well, that settles it then, doesn't it, dear?" said the Countess, cocking her head toward her husband. "Dear Granville must have accidentally consumed something that caused the poisoning. That must be the explanation."

A murmur of faint agreement arose from the table, though no one person assented openly. It was a convenient way for them to be in denial, thought Fina. Because the alternative was too uncomfortable to contemplate.

19

After lunch, the guests moved together, en masse, to the saloon. Fina detected an undercurrent of fear, though on the surface everyone clung to a superficial normalcy. Many family members were absent – Charlotte had retired to her room with one of her regularly scheduled headaches, and the Countess said she would attend to her fish. She said she found them soothing. As for Edgar, Grimston had helped him to his room for his sure-to-be-impending hangover headache. Only the Earl stayed on with the guests, determined to carry on with the Yuletide spirit.

Ruby had said she was sleepy and needed a nap. Fina doubted that. They had been separated at lunchtime so they were not able to compare notes, as it were, after everyone had left the dining room. Besides, Charles had pulled her aside to tell her that they would have to postpone their meeting. Charles... she thought dreamily about him. She shook herself. There was sleuthing to be done.

Gayatri, Ian and Julia took up cards at a large table in the centre of the saloon. Fina had been invited to join. She nearly accepted – thinking she might instigate some more gossiping –

but decided against it as she wanted to talk to Ruby soon. Somehow the terrible events of this morning had smoothed over the edges of tension between the threesome she had witnessed last night. Soon bored of the initial game, they moved on to a rather serious game of bridge. Every time Julia's pair won a rubber, she let out a whoop of delight. Must be the need to focus on something.

Sajida flipped through the latest *Vogue*, pettishly. She gave out a sigh, looking up at the window where the hail had turned back into the omnipresent snow.

Ever the professor, Cyril, sat in the corner, reading Carl Schmitt's *The Concept of the Political*. His forehead wrinkled in concentration, though Fina noticed he never turned the pages of the book. Was he contemplating complicated political philosophy or something else?

The Earl, after trying and failing to engage Cyril in conversation, sat in an enormous plush mauve chair near the window, smoking a cigar. Must have been one of the Countess' purchases, she thought. He looked like he was sitting in the arms of a large, pink elephant. He gazed out the window, occasionally peering at the foul-smelling cigar as if it were a fascinating object. The next time she looked in his direction, she could see his eyes closed and moustache gently rippling from his snorts and grunts.

Time to get on with it, Fina told herself.

Her favourite ivory shoes echoed so loudly on the stone floor in the hallway that she felt forced to tiptoe rather than disturb the silence. As she passed the study – where the door had been open a crack – she saw something flash across the room. She crept up to the door still on tiptoe and peeked in through the opening. She could see a forest-green-brocaded figure huddling over one of the bookcases in the corner. Only one person wore that rich brocade – Charlotte. And the bookcase was where the testimony had been kept.

Fina moved her feet backwards, carefully and quietly. Then something squirmed around her ankle. She tumbled backwards, tripping, and caught herself on the opposite wall, but not before thrashing about with the umbrella stand nearby. The cat! Grayling looked offended by Fina's lack of grace. The door opened and out came Charlotte.

"Are you all right, Fina?" she said, reaching out to steady her arm. Charlotte's face was flushed. Her dress, always a perfect fit, was somehow askew, though Fina could not pinpoint why it appeared so.

"Yes, yes, I'm fine, thank you," Fina replied, patting her hair back into place – or at least out of her face. The two women stared at each other, both embarrassed – as if guilty of some-thing – though each apparently uncertain as to if they had any real reason to be. "I'm afraid I tripped over the cat. I was going up to my room and I thought I'd find a book in the library to read before a short nap," said Fina. "I was just on my way there."

Charlotte's eyes lit up. Was it because Fina had provided a convenient cover story for her own snooping?

"Ah, yes, I–I, I was in the study myself for the same reason. I thought I would read to take my mind off... things," she said, swinging her arms to emphasize the casualness of her endeavour.

"Did you find anything?" asked Fina, proud of herself for the sufficiently vague phrasing of the question. "I mean, wouldn't the library rather than the study be a better place to find a book?"

"Find anything? Oh – you mean a book. I couldn't find anything that sparked my interest so I was just getting ready to return to my bedroom. I didn't bother with the library. It's, it's –

there are so many of Auntie's fish in there that I feel I might knock over a fishbowl if I search for a book. I think I'll be on my way now," she said, tipping her head to the side just a bit to motion toward the stairs. She hurried off.

20

"Ruby...." said Fina, now sitting comfortably in front of the fireplace in Ruby's room.

"Mmm, yes, Feens?" she said, busily scribbling away in her notebook.

"I was just in the library and Charlotte was acting rather oddly."

"Odd in what way?"

Scratching her head, she said, "Her dress was askew. Now that wouldn't be out of the norm for most of us, but for perfect Charlotte? And she had come out of the study looking rather sheepish, as if I had caught her in a rather sticky situation."

"Superior sleuthing skills, my friend," said Ruby glancing up from the page. "I've just made note of her behaviour in my little notebook."

"While we're on the subject of things that don't quite fit, I've just been thinking about the photograph in Edgar's room yesterday. It was of Edgar and his mother – I presume it was his mother. They both looked very happy. The reason I noticed it – besides the look of joy on their faces, was that there was something odd about it. Not the photo... but the placement of it. It was the only photo in the room and you definitely noticed it," said Fina, with a vacant look. When Fina had first met Ruby, she had had to tell her that her frozen-squirrel-stare was the result of accelerated brain activity.

"What's odd about a family photo on a desk?" asked Ruby. "I mean, the Earl, Countess and Sykes-Duckworths don't strike me as particularly affectionate when it comes to family – but that's no different than the rest of the English aristocracy," she said, ending in an acid tone.

"Yes, that's true – perhaps that's just it. First of all, their open display of joy was remarkable precisely because they're reserved when it comes to affection. It was also located in an odd place. Not by the bedside table – as many photos are in bedrooms. It was almost as if it were positioned as some sort of altar or shrine," said Fina.

"Well, we did learn from the cook that their mother died young, correct? It's not surprising, then, that he would have some sort of altar-esque setup. But the fact that you noticed it means something, Fina. Let's write it down," she said, doing just that with an efficient scribble in her notebook.

"By the way," said Fina, remembering her confusion after lunch, "why did you say you wanted to take a nap? You left me all alone in there!"

"Oh, of course. I'm so sorry. I remembered a spot in my room where I thought the poison could be, so I wanted to hurry back to search – and I didn't have time to tell you why. I was unsuccessful, obviously. I figured you could continue sleuthing without me, which you obviously did quite well!"

Looking contrite, Ruby rose from the bed and rummaged around in her bag. She held up a small box in triumph. Grinning, she removed the top, ran it under her nose so she could smell it lightly, and then held it out to Fina.

Fina gasped with delight. "Fuller's chocolates! You've been

holding out on me!" she said with a laugh, instantly feeling the mood lighten. Nestled in lavender papers, each individual chocolate gleamed like pirates' treasure, thought Fina. There were few things in life that made her happier than a box of Fuller's chocolates.

"Mhhh..." said Ruby, sinking her teeth into one of the soft chunks. Shifting the papers aside with her fingers, Fina finally settled on the selection of a perfect sphere sprinkled with nuts.

"That's much better," pronounced Fina. "Now I will be able to concentrate. Right. Shall we start with opportunity?"

Ruby nodded. "Yes, though we still have the problem of the missing poison. I suppose we'll have to assume it was in either the snifter or the cocoa cup for now."

"So we're left with Edgar, possibly Cyril – if he was able to put something in the snifter just before he left. As for the cocoa, it could be Julia, Ian, the cook, Charles, Grimston and any of the staff."

"Yes – and don't forget ourselves," winked Ruby.

"Yes, of course. Another reason we have to solve this mystery as soon as possible," said Fina, scribbling away in the notebook. Something nagged at her about the poison. Study... snifter... opportunity.

"What is it, Fina? Did you remember something important?" asked Ruby.

"It's probably nothing, but it was peculiar. Remember when we were in the study – searching for the papers – I noticed a large wet spot on the carpet next to the French windows? It was odd because it was recent and quite large," said Fina.

Ruby leaned forward, swallowing her second chocolate – not that Fina was counting, of course. "I do remember – we thought it might be from the snow."

"Yes," said Fina, absently. "Do you think someone poured

out a snifter of brandy in a rush? Maybe they couldn't dispose of it anywhere else. In normal weather you could simply open the windows and chuck it out, but not now," she said, shivering as she glanced at the window.

"Yes... Perhaps our murderer needed to dispose of the brandy."

"Which brandy – the poison snifter or one just normal brandy?" asked Fina.

"Assuming the poison was oxalic acid, I know from my own use of it that it does not dissolve quickly. You need to stir it up a bit. That means that if you were going to slip poison into a brandy snifter, you'd have to prepare it beforehand, and it would need to dissolve in at least a half of a brandy snifter of liquid. Even if you had a flask prepared beforehand that you could pour into unsuspecting Granville's glass when he wasn't looking, you'd still need to dispose of the original brandy somehow because it would be too obvious that the glass was suddenly full," said Ruby, moving full speed ahead.

"Yes, unless you could count on Granville being blotto and therefore in no condition to notice," said Fina.

"That's true, but you couldn't plan on that for sure. This was a premeditated murder – or at least premeditated in the sense that it wasn't a split-second reaction. It had to have been planned out at least an hour or so in advance. More or less between the time I made the announcement over cocktails about the stain remover and then when he was slipped the poison," said Ruby.

"Couldn't the murderer just put the poison in their own glass and then switch it with Granville's glass?" asked Fina.

"Good point, but the problem is what happens if you are forced to a toast before you're able to make the switch? Too risky. See how this strikes you: the murderer, holding a snifter, makes some excuse to leave the study, because he or she wouldn't be able to empty the flask into anyone's glass – including his or her own – without being seen. They search for a place to discard the ordinary brandy. The best they can do is that mat by the door in another room, knowing that it will likely dry by the morning. Besides, since it's near a door, no one will think twice about it. Then they open the flask, empty it into the snifter and then return to the study, where they make a quick switch with Granville's snifter." She pursed her lips, mulling over her own story, moving her eyes from side to side.

"But why not just chuck the lot into the fireplace?" asked Fina. "It would be harder to detect."

"Perhaps, but since we know there wasn't a fire in the study in the evening, it would flare up the next time someone lit a fire. Maybe it would rouse suspicion. I don't know, Feens... it's also odd because I doubt the rug would stay wet overnight from just a glassful of brandy."

"Good point. Regardless of that spot on the rug, though, we still have a good theory running about the vehicle for the poison. So for my notes – assuming the poison was put in the brandy rather than the cocoa, that means the murder had to be either Cyril or Edgar since they were the only ones who were around to put the poison in the flask. At least in terms of the time of the murder," said Fina, head bent as she scribbled furiously. They had traded the role of note-taking scribe.

"Cyril or Edgar. I suppose so, even though I am unsatisfied with the plausibility of the story," Ruby said, shrugging her shoulders as she continued. "Now we come to the cocoa. If it were the cocoa, then our suspects are Ian and Julia, correct? We can eliminate the staff for now unless Charles tells us otherwise."

"So that means our suspect list is Cyril, Edgar, Julia and Ian. It still doesn't seem quite right, but let's review the clues we have thus far," said Fina. "There's the papers I found in Edgar's room, which suggest Lavington's were planning some sort of corporate raid on their competition. That may implicate Gayatri and Sajida's family."

"Possibly," said Ruby, tapping her teeth. "Then there's the question of what happens to Pauncefort after Lord Malvern dies. I've heard he's not too well."

"That gives all of the family a motive, though most likely the Earl and Countess. I cannot imagine them murdering anyone, much less their own relative."

"I cannot really imagine any of them doing it, but don't forget that Granville himself was a murderer, even if he didn't pull the trigger himself," said Ruby softly.

"That's so true," said Fina, letting the moment sit in silence. "What about that flare up between Julia, Ian and Gayatri last night in the saloon? Remember the looks they gave one another? What about a love triangle angle?" Fina stopped, remembering the chummy atmosphere between the three of them in the saloon. "They seemed to have patched it up this afternoon, though. They were enjoying playing cards – just the three of them."

"Hmm... it could have seemed more serious than it really was last night – remember we're dealing with theatrical types. I also know Julia finds anything that moves attractive, so that means we could have a many pointed star rather than a simple triangle," said Ruby, eyes twinkling.

"Speaking of that, did you notice how red Leslie's eyes were at lunch today? He seems to be the only one who really mourned Granville at all. And I must say they were very close..."

"You're thinking how close, aren't you? Well, it's certainly plausible. I feel like someone did hint at it yesterday, though I cannot remember when," said Fina. She flounced back on the bed in exhaustion. Looking up at the ceiling, she said, "Yes, if that's true, though, why would he kill his lover? Seems like he'd be more likely to kill someone else vying for his attention."

"I suppose, but it could have been out of jealousy, or fear of someone discovering the truth... Oh Fina, we're in the soup. We have a list of suspects, but it's all still so vague. I hope the snow stops soon – but please, dear Lord, not before we find the killer."

21

"Has anyone seen Mr Dashwood?" enquired the Countess.

Assembled in the drawing room for afternoon tea, the guests sat around a table with mounds of untouched sandwiches and small cakes. Fina noticed the level of dress matched the tone of the gathering this time – more subdued. The most flamboyant dresser of the bunch, Julia, lounged in a rather muted wine-coloured velvet vest arrangement, a smoking jacket without sleeves.

The burning Christmas candles along the perimeter of the room struck Fina as a defiant gesture – that the festivities should continue. Surely this was at the behest of the Earl, but she found it hard to reconcile this attention to detail with the tragedy of murder. Perhaps it was just his way of coping.

Fina felt slightly guilty that she had enjoyed a luxurious bath before tea, relishing the water that was actually hot – something she never had in college. She had taken her time dressing, feeling more confident in herself for some reason. She felt less intimidated by the other guests since she knew some of their secrets now.

Surveying the body language of the guests in response to the

Countess' enquiry, she noticed a definite tightening of muscles and straightening of postures. Everyone tried to look casual – everyone, that is, except for Sajida who had a look of terror in her eyes. Fina guessed this was because she was already on edge due to her sister's earlier vanishing act.

Everyone looked at one another, askance. No one spoke. Finally, Ian cleared his throat. "I saw Mr Dashwood in the library, sitting by the fire. That was perhaps an hour ago."

Silence. Ian continued, "Has anyone else see him since that time?" A few heads shook. The question hung in the air.

Plop, plop. A small avalanche of snow cascaded past the window, streaks of white against the dark windowpane. Fina jumped. The image of Granville's body, motionless on the bed, came unbidden to her mind.

Lady Charlotte turned to Grimston. "Please go to Mr Dashwood's room and knock. Take Charles with you in case... in case..." she trailed off, waving her handkerchief in the direction of the exit.

Ruby floated over to Charlotte and whispered in her ear. Charlotte nodded and said, "Miss Dove has a helpful suggestion. Let us split into pairs and search the lower floors to see if he's fallen asleep somewhere."

"Right. The man's a waster and a drunk, so he's probably passed out somewhere," mumbled Ian.

Everyone tacitly agreed with Ruby's suggestion by pairing off as if they were going to a formal dance. Ruby and Fina waited behind until other guests trickled out of the drawing room.

"Any luck?"

Fina and Ruby spun round at the voice from the doorway. Gayatri had returned, alone.

"Luck?" said Fina, quickly realizing she meant luck finding the absent Leslie. "Ah, no. But since you're here, may we ask you a question?"

"Of course," said Gayatri with alacrity, though she crossed her arms in front of her. She seemed to sink into the door frame.

"Sajida is visiting from Tezpur, correct?" asked Ruby.

"Yes."

"Are any of your family members from Nowgong – originally?" enquired Fina.

Gayatri's eyes narrowed. "What is this about, exactly?" Despite her defiance, Fina thought she detected a note of fear.

"I'll be direct, Gayatri—" said Ruby.

"Yes, please do. I do want to know what this sudden interest in my family is all about."

"We've seen some papers here that related to Nowgong. And Lavington's." Ruby paused for effect. Fina stared at her friend in admiration. Her friend's lightning-quick wit and ability to bend the truth came to the rescue – for the sake of justice, of course.

Ruby continued, "We're fairly certain that the Sykes-Duckworths – the family behind Lavington's – also own a tea plantation in Nowgong. We couldn't help but think about the connection when we found out that Sajida was visiting from a town near there... Perhaps that is your original connection with the Sykes-Duckworths, rather than Oxford?"

Gayatri gave out a sigh and moved to sit on a settee near the door. She slumped down, looking defeated. "Yes, there is a connection. You see, our family was, or I should say is, royalty near Nowgong. Dulcet & Sons owns plantations near there. There have been a number of local rebellions by the tea workers. We want the British out. Dulcet is prepared to go bankrupt – at least in that area. That's why they're ready to sell up to Lavington's at a cut-rate price. Tea companies are notoriously brutal, but Lavington's has a horrific track record that sets them apart. They are unlikely to let go, even if they lose money, once they get their hands on this area."

"Is this the real reason you and your sister came down here

this weekend?" asked Fina, feeling like it came out more bluntly than she had intended.

Gayatri clenched her fist, but her face remained impassive. "Yes, it looks that way. We really came down here on a whim. I suppose we thought we could convince Granville, or someone in the family could convince Granville, not to buy out Dulcet & Sons. We didn't have any sort of plan. It was just an impulse. I was against it at first, but you see how impulsive Sajida is."

"Impulsive enough to commit murder?" asked Ruby, quietly.

"She is impulsive, but that drives her to make poor decisions about raising her voice at someone or spending too much money, not planning to slip poison in a glass of brandy or a cup of cocoa. If she were to kill someone – which I'm not saying she would – it would be completely spontaneous. If there were even a ten-minute interval between the impulse and the action, she wouldn't be able to do it."

"But Gayatri, that leaves... you," murmured Fina, feeling awful even as she said it.

Silence. Ruby and Fina remained frozen, as if moving would turn off the stream of Gayatri's explanations.

This seemed to work, as Gayatri took a deep breath and continued. "If I had planned to murder Granville, it would have been *planned* and I would have made sure no one would have discovered me. Besides, I was the only one who could tell you for certain that he had been poisoned. If I had poisoned him, I simply would have said he died of natural causes."

"Assuming that's a plausible explanation," said Ruby, "who do *you* think committed the murder?"

"Well, the only person who has a nasty enough personality – at least from outward appearances – is Leslie Dashwood. But now that he's missing..."

At that moment, there was a commotion in the hallway. The

three women moved quickly out of the drawing room. A small group had assembled with the Countess at the helm.

"He's... he's... dead?" said the Countess, her whole body quivering like a slow-onset earthquake.

"It does appear so, milady. The gentleman has expired," said Grimston in a calm, officious manner, though his forehead was glistening with sweat.

"Expired, expired?" boomed the Earl. "Good God, man, we're not talking about the milk being off. What happened?"

"It appears, sir, that Mr Dashwood died in a similar manner to Master Granville," said Charles, breathless from running downstairs. "We found him, prostrate, on the carpet in his room. He had dressed for dinner. He had a similar... ah... discolouration on his cheek as Master Granville. The door to his bedroom was locked, as was the outside bathroom door. The door between the bedroom and the adjoining bathroom was open, however."

Gayatri stepped forward. "I'd like to examine the body again, if I may, Earl and Countess. I'd also like to ask Miss Dove and Miss Aubrey-Havelock to accompany me, as they inspected the first... ah... scene."

"Is that wise, Lord and Lady Snittlegarth?" asked Cyril, casting a sharp glance at the two women. He likes to be in control, thought Fina.

"Professor Lighton, anything that will help us get to the heart of this tragedy is welcome. Please do proceed, Miss Dove, Miss Aubrey-Havelock and Miss Badarur," said the Countess, invoking her rarely-invoked imperious tone, nodding toward the women.

22

The broken door, askew on its hinges, provided a sad welcome to the bedroom. Sprawled on a beautiful antique rug, the body of Leslie Dashwood lay face down – positioned between the door to the bathroom and the large four-poster bed in the middle of the room. Fina nearly gagged at the sour odour permeating the room.

Gayatri and Charles immediately knelt down near Leslie. Charles gently rolled the body back so Gayatri could look at the face. "Yes, it's the same signs of acid-related trauma. Could be the same type of poison. Hard to say for certain," she said.

As Gayatri and Charles continued to examine the body, Ruby and Fina agreed to make a thorough search of the room. "Maybe we'll find something that will help us piece this together," said Ruby.

They agreed to search the perimeter of the room in separate directions and then place their findings on a small lacquer table near the door. It was strange, thought Fina, how a quiet corpse could generate such a beehive of activity.

Task completed, they had amassed what looked like a museum exhibit of artefacts on the small table. Just like any museum curator worth her salt, Fina sat down with her notebook to catalogue the items.

Ruby selected each item, in turn, and described them in hushed tones for Fina's notes.

"One book. Oswald Mosley's *The Greater Britain*." Ruby's eyebrow raised. "The inscription reads, 'To my one and only'.

"That's it? No initial or signature?" asked Fina.

"No, unfortunately. But it could be Granville's handwriting, given our theory. Perhaps we can find a sample later," said Ruby, as she picked up the next item for the catalogue.

"Next, we have a small box of mints... empty," Ruby said, shaking it and placing it back on the table. "One handkerchief, unused, but by the bedside. One clean notepad and pen. One leather toiletry case." She unzipped the pale grey case to reveal a number of items. "Quite the groomer, Mr Dashwood. One small leather case with scissors, and an assortment of tweezers and files. One clothes brush, one ebony mirror, one shaving brush container, with the shaving brush, one shaving container with lid – and cream. One toothbrush holder, empty. One comb. That's the lot."

"I looked through all of the pockets in his wardrobe and didn't find anything of interest," said Fina.

Gesturing at the array of items on the table, Ruby said, "So what does this tell us, besides the fact—" she lowered her voice even further "—that Leslie may have been on intimate terms with Granville?"

"Could Leslie have killed Granville – perhaps a jealous rage of some sort – and then killed himself? Or maybe he murdered Granville and then whomever was part of this love triangle, or love star, as you said, killed him for revenge?" surmised Fina.

"I suppose that's possible, though something about this doesn't add up to a suicide – either in his case or in Granville's. There's no note, either. And there's too many murderers in the other scenario. No..." Ruby tapped the table with the pen. "Let's ask ourselves a question about this room."

Fina settled herself back in her chair so she could have a panoramic view of the room.

"Besides the peculiar position of the body – though what normal means in these circumstances, I cannot imagine – what is odd?" asked Ruby, scanning the room.

"Odd? What do you mean by odd?" asked Fina.

"Perhaps odd isn't the right word. I believe I mean to say, what's missing? Given what we know about Leslie Dashwood, what's missing?"

"Alcohol," said Fina, firmly and quickly. She surprised herself with how quickly the image of the drunken Leslie came into her mind.

"Exactly," agreed Ruby. "We haven't seen Leslie without a drink this entire weekend, except perhaps at breakfast. But even then, who knows?" she said, the corner of her mouth lifting into a sardonic grin. "The point is that there is no evidence of a vehicle for ingesting the poison."

"Yes, you've hit upon it," said Fina excitedly. "It's the exact opposite – though the method was the same – from Granville's murder. There were too many receptacles – or vehicles as you say – to deliver the poison in that case, though there's no evidence of poison residue. In this case, where is the glass or cup – or even flask – that contained the poison?"

"Charles," said Fina, rising to walk toward the body where Gayatri and Charles were talking quietly. "Did you see any sort of glass or cup when you and Grimston entered the room? It's important because there doesn't seem to be any evidence of a way for Leslie to have taken the poison."

"No, I would have noticed – since I'm trained to look for those sorts of things to tidy up. I'm sure Grimston wouldn't have removed anything in any case – especially not after it was so clear that it was murder... this time," said Charles. He then held out his clenched hand and opened it. "We've searched his pockets and found this."

Fina picked up the gold necklace, a delicate oval locket with a broken chain. The surface of the locket had an elaborate engraving with the initial C. Prying it open with rising excitement, Fina found the locket was empty.

"Charlotte is the only obvious person this could belong to – or be a present for, though it looks rather ancient, like an heirloom," said Ruby. "How about middle names: do any of the women here have a middle initial C?"

"I don't know about the guests, but I do know that Lady Snittlegarth's middle initial is C for Charlotte as well. Charlotte is named after Lady Snittlegarth," said Charles.

"What about you, Gayatri, and your sister?" asked Ruby.

Gayatri shook her head, but continued, "And for the record, what about the two of you, Ruby and Fina?" Ruby and Fina looked at one another and let out a light laugh.

"I apologize, Charles and Gayatri, I think it must be the shock getting to us. My full name is Ruby Betto Dove," said Ruby, turning to Fina.

"My full name is Fina Siobhan Aubrey-Havelock," said Fina, recovering herself.

"Doesn't Siobhan start with a C?" asked Charles.

"It's Irish, Charles. It's spelled S-i-o-b-h-a-n," said Fina with a smile, not wanting to make Charles feel inadequate.

"Of course, of course," said Charles, reddening.

"Well, we have quite a list of clues, now, don't we?" said Ruby. "Besides confirming where everyone was in the past few hours, we need to find out who the mysterious C represents. And we also need to find a copy of Granville's handwriting."

As Charles and Gayatri left the room, Ruby made as if to follow them, but once they were out of earshot, she turned and motioned to Fina to go into the bathroom. They entered the narrow room, covered in a luscious jade green tile with a large claw-foot bath. A towel hung on a rack near the door. There was a medicine cabinet and a mirror with a washbasin near the door. As one would expect, thought Fina, there was a soap dish with a bar of soap, as well as a toothbrush perched precariously on the edge of the sink.

Ruby felt the inside bottom of the bath and then the towel. "Wet," she said. Then she opened the cabinet. It contained a tin of tooth powder and a jar of pomade. Frowning, she turned to Fina. "I thought there might be a glass in here, but I don't see one anywhere, do you?"

Shaking her head in agreement, Fina followed Ruby back out to the bedroom. "You were right to look in the bathroom – it looks as if he fell as he was walking out. Do you think he was poisoned in there?"

"It's clear that he had to have ingested the poison somewhere in this bedroom or bathroom. He would not have enough time to drink something downstairs, walk up the stairs, take a bath, get dressed, go back into the bathroom and then..." Ruby froze. "And then..." she said to herself, staring at the ceiling.

She trotted back into the bathroom. "Feens!" she yelled. "Look at this," she said, returning to the bedroom, toothbrush in hand. "Feel it."

Fina whisked her finger over the top of the toothbrush. "Yes, it's wet. So? He brushed his teeth."

Ruby stared back at her. Fina could see she was willing her to see the light.

Fina blinked.

"It would be the only thing that he put in his mouth... and therefore must be the way he was poisoned," said Ruby.

Ruby continued, grasping Fina's arm for what seemed to be intellectual and physical support. "That explains how Granville was poisoned, too. It would be too risky to put it on the tooth-brush itself – it might be noticed."

"Or rinsed before brushing," said Fina, happy she was able to make however small a contribution to Ruby's deductive chain of logic.

"So it must be the tooth powder," said Ruby as she moved back into the bathroom to retrieve the tooth powder. She sniffed the toothbrush delicately. "Yes, it's there all right – just a trace, but very distinctive. Would you go to Granville's bathroom to find the toothbrush and tooth powder? That is, assuming the murderer didn't take it already."

23

Fina glided down the hallway, trying her best to appear causal – nay insouciant – should she confront any unexpected guests on her way to Granville's bathroom. She threw back her shoulders and held up her chin, imagining she was modelling clothes in a fashion parade at one of the grand houses in Paris.

Her foray into fantasy fashion modelling came to an abrupt halt when she nearly tripped on a curled bit of rug outside a bathroom door. The bathroom created an echo chamber effect, so she could hear voices wafting in from the adjoining bedroom. It was Julia's room. Fina leaned in through the bathroom doorway. The door was ajar, so she thought it only fair game – this was murder after all – to listen.

She could recognize Julia's voice, quavering. "I can't believe he's gone..."

Then Sajida said in a hushed tone, "Yes... he won't bother us any more."

Fina heard footsteps approaching. She dashed around the corner. To confirm her voice recognition, she saw Sajida creep out of the door – looking both ways – before she descended the stairs to her room. Fina's mind raced, trying to figure out what the conversation could possibly mean. Plenty of time to think that over later, she told herself.

She crept along the hallway to Granville's room, trying not to think about what lay inside. This was no time for nerves. Pushing lightly on the door, she averted her gaze from the bed, where the body still lay, shrouded in a sheet. Perhaps she would be able to sidle all the way to the bathroom without laying eyes on it. Fina had never been superstitious, but one of her great-aunts used to swear that there was no better cure for gout or fever than the touch of a dead man's hand – an image that had given her nightmares as a child. Her shoulders wobbled in an involuntary shudder.

Facing the wall, she crept carefully toward the bathroom door. She stepped back to avoid bumping her hip on a small burr-walnut desk that was pushed into the corner of the room, but then her eye was caught by a note thrown carelessly down on the blotting-pad.

28th Oct. Burlington meet. Wet. A doe raised in Loughdown wood. Tracked her Woolton way, over rough ground, and through Parker's spinney. Hounds lost scent at the bank of the Rye.

3rd Nov. Airesdale meet. Wet, cold. A hind had been harboured in the copse by Braisedale farm. He circled, then led us up Fieldston way, where we lost him. He was fresh put up east of Woolton and we brought him down by the fallow field. A good day's hunting.

Repressing a sad thought for the deer, Fina focused on the handwriting. Surely it was the same as the hand on the flyleaf of the book Ruby had found in Leslie's room. She pocketed the paper, silently thanking Ruby yet again for those miraculous pockets, and edged her way into the bathroom.

The layout was the same as Leslie's bathroom on the lower

floor; the only difference here was the brilliant azure tile. With a rapid step, she went over to the washbasin and medicine cabinet. No tooth powder. The murderer must have removed it sometime after the crime, she thought. The toothbrush was there, however. Perhaps there would be residue on the brush. With a satisfied grin of accomplishment, she inserted it in the small red clutch she carried under her arm, along with her leather notebook.

A sudden flash of motion, reflected in the mirror, made her look up. Was there someone there? Turning, she peered around the hallway. Nothing. All was serene. And yet she felt sure she hadn't imagined it. Then, without warning, she felt a thud on the base of her skull.

24

"Feens, Fina!"

"Can you speak to us, Fina?"

"Mmmhhph…" mumbled Fina in return. She blinked up at the two concerned faces. Ruby's hair was perfect, as usual, in contrast to Charles. Even in her stupor she could appreciate the rakish charm of his dishevelled nearly-ebony hair.

"This place is a madhouse," said Charles, more to himself than to Ruby or Fina. "When I find the person that did this, I'll…"

Ruby said gently, "No need for heroics, Charles. We need to get Fina comfortable and away from this scene."

Each taking one end of Fina – Fina couldn't help but have peculiar images of herself as a corpse when they did this – they lumbered awkwardly, but carefully down the stairs. Charles leaned against Fina's door to open it and they soon had ensconced her in the comfortable bed. After checking her head and giving her some water, Ruby said, "We'll leave you for now, Fina, so you can rest. I'll be right here, reading, to make sure nothing happens."

"I'm groggy, Ruby, but I don't want to rest. I can't – not with a murderer on the loose. Especially now that they seem to be coming after me," said Fina. She looked at Charles. "Please don't leave, either. You two are the only ones I can really trust, so let's discuss this together."

Ruby flashed her a warning look. Fina nodded, almost imperceptibly to let her know she understood.

"Let's start at the beginning," said Ruby.

Fina snorted, then winced. "Have you found out who hit me?"

"No, unfortunately. There was no one there by the time we arrived."

"Blast! If only I'd looked up at the right moment, I'd have seen his reflection."

"Or hers," Charles added. "Did you find the toothbrush before you were hit on the head?" asked Charles.

Fina rubbed her head, trying to remember. "Yes, I think so." She pointed at the clutch she had been carrying. Ruby opened it, rummaged around and shook her head.

"Did you find out anything else before you were attacked?" asked Ruby. Fina proceeded to tell them about her eavesdropping in the hallway. She left out the bit about tripping on the rug.

"That does seem to cast a new light on Julia and Sajida's relationship," said Charles, reddening. "I didn't even think they had met each other before this weekend."

"Neither did we," said Ruby. "It is suggestive. I want to follow up this bit about the toothpaste, though, before I lose my line of thought. We can assume the method of poisoning was the same in both cases. Poison in the tooth powder or toothbrush. Most likely in the tooth powder since the murderer couldn't know if the Granville or Leslie would rinse their toothbrush before using the powder."

Charles said, "Usually you wet it first, so it wouldn't be fool-proof to put it on the toothbrush."

Ruby nodded, rose and began to pace back and forth in front of Fina's merrily crackling fire.

"So it must have been the tooth powder. This information means we have to throw everyone's initial alibis out the window. Or," Ruby said, looking out at the mounds of white snow glowing dimly in the dark landscape, "into the fireplace, as it were. The murderer may have planned to kill Granville in advance, but they couldn't have known about my stain remover."

"Do you think they just seized the opportunity when you announced it in the drawing room?" asked Fina.

"They must have," said Ruby. "Is there another alternative?" she said, plaintively looking at Charles and Fina who returned her look as if they were puppies who had failed to please their owner.

"Oof," said Fina, touching her head. Charles rushed over to her, helplessly trying to rearrange pillows as if that would make a difference. She appreciated the effort, however.

"Please, continue, Ruby. I'm fine."

Ruby reached over to pat her feet gently and continued. "That means that someone must have gone to my room and then put the poison in Granville's tooth powder between the time I returned from my room after cleaning Gayatri's dress and then before Granville went up to bed."

She turned to Charles. "How long do you think it would take to leave one of the ground floor rooms – the drawing room, dining room, library, study, or saloon – go to my room and then to Granville's room? We also have to take into account the time it would take to find the poison in my room. I left it out on my dresser so it wouldn't take more than a few minutes."

Charles scratched his head. "I'd say the total round trip would take fifteen minutes at a minimum, plus the time to find the poison – as you said – and to put it in Granville's tooth powder. That would take an additional five minutes, assuming the murderer knew exactly what they'd be doing."

"So the murderer was absent for a minimum of twenty minutes," said Fina. "That's an awfully long time to be gone in the lavatory that is near the dining hall on the ground floor."

"Yes, the absence would definitely be noticed," said Ruby with a grin.

"I had a word with Mrs Lynn, as you asked me to," said Charles, "and she told me Charlotte spent at least a quarter of an hour with her in the pantry after dinner, discussing the menus. So that seems to be on the level."

"Possibly... although it seemed to me that she was gone for much longer than that," said Ruby reflectively.

"What about the second murder?" asked Charles.

"The placing of the poison in Leslie's bathroom must have occurred well after breakfast. Otherwise, given what we know now about Leslie, he most likely brushed his teeth before or immediately following breakfast and would have died much earlier," said Ruby. "I think Leslie must have found out something that made the murderer nervous."

"He had been crying and was rather broody," said Fina. "Though I suppose we all chalked that up to the death of his lover."

Charles' eyes grew wide. "Do you mean... No. That can't be."

Oh dear, thought Fina. That may have been a bit too badly put. She pulled out the hunt report from her pocket and brandished it at Charles.

"This is Granville's hand, is it not?" she asked. "We found a book in Leslie's room with a rather, er, intimate inscription. In the same hand. There can be no doubt about it."

"*Lover*?" Charles made an effort to rally. "I–I–well. That is certainly his hand, but... Ah. Um," he trailed off, wiping his brow.

Blithely ignoring his shock, Ruby continued. "Let's assume that something was said during or after breakfast that made the murderer act. It's much more difficult to fix alibis for everyone because that's such a long period of time between breakfast and his death."

"If we focus on his movements, specifically, then we might be able to track when there were windows of opportunity. I can ask the staff to find out if we can piece this together," said Charles in a steady voice, despite his shocked countenance.

Ruby nodded in gratitude. "That will be helpful. Thank you." As she said this, Fina noticed that Ruby stood still. Her hands were in her pockets and she looked like a schoolmistress ready to dismiss her pupils. Fina took the hint.

"Charles, would you be so kind as to bring me some tea and toast. I think that would help me feel better. You could also interview the staff on the way back – so no rush," said Fina, looking up at him adoringly.

"Of course, Fina," he said gently brushing his hand against hers as he rose to leave.

25

"We'll talk about the two of you later," said Ruby with a laugh. "Now that he's gone we can move on to discussing the suspects!"

Ruby pulled out her notebook and drew a neat vertical line down the middle of a page. She wrote the names of Granville and Leslie at the top of each column. "Let's review motives for each murder. I'll start with Leslie."

"Why Leslie? Isn't he the victim? Or did my head injury cause memory loss?"

"Well, if we assume Leslie committed suicide, then it's plausible he committed the first murder. It goes like this: he kills Granville because of something having to do with their relationship – maybe Granville threatened to tell someone about it, or maybe it was jealousy. Maybe Granville was in love with someone else and Leslie killed him, felt terrible remorse, and then did himself in."

Fina began to warm to the subject. She sat up a bit more in bed. "That's plausible. It's also plausible – following the same line – that Leslie was killed because Granville's other lover discovered Leslie had done the deed – and then the other lover sought revenge. Rather sordid, though."

"Ra-ther," said Ruby with a grimace. "Let's stay with this for a minute though. Mind you, I'm just talking this through aloud. What about the timing of the murders? Is there any chance *Granville* actually murdered Leslie rather than vice versa? What I mean is that Granville puts the poison in both tooth powders, assuming that Leslie will take it at around the same time."

Fina sighed. "You're ingenious, Ruby." She stared into the fire for a moment. "I suppose it's possible, but the timing seems off. Given what we now know about Leslie, it seems unlikely that he didn't brush his teeth at bedtime or at breakfast."

"It does seem unlikely. You're right. We'll assume some sort of love-interest complication for Leslie and that he wanted to make his suicide look like murder – either because he didn't want the truth of their affair to come out or because he wanted to cast suspicion on someone else."

"Who's next on our list?" asked Fina.

Flipping the page and smoothing out a new, clean writing surface, Ruby said, "Julia. We've been through her difficulties with Granville already, though the conversation you overheard before you were attacked seems to indicate some sort of love triangle—"

"Love star," said Fina with a grin.

"Quite," said Ruby, returning the grin. "You're rather lucid for someone with a head injury."

Touching her head as if she had forgotten the injury – and then wincing – Fina continued. "It could have been that Julia was just comforting Sajida as a friend, but the tone definitely made it seem like more than that."

Ruby tapped her teeth with the pencil. "Sajida could have killed one or both of them. She's rather a mystery, you know. She's meant to be here to revel in the atmosphere of a grand old traditional English Christmas, but every time I catch sight of her, she looks bored to tears."

Fina had slid back under the silky covers, so she sat up a little more in bed, but her head started to swim. She nestled back further into the pillows. "What if Granville was protecting Leslie in some way, and he was killed to keep him quiet? That would be really devious. Make it appear the target is Granville when it's really Leslie."

"Devious indeed! I cannot see how anyone would have a reason to kill Leslie, unless it was something to do with his relationship with Granville. Still, you might have something when you say he could have been killed to keep him quiet. He certainly wasn't the type to hold his tongue."

"Especially after a few too many brandy-and-sodas," Fina added, remembering her painful encounter with him the day before.

"He may have had some involvement with Lavington's that we're unaware of. Those papers in Edgar's desk were hardly confidential; anyone could have seen them. And that includes Sajida and her sister. I know Gayatri told us they only came here to talk things over with Granville, but can we believe them?"

If they're the ones who asked you to hand over the Bluegate papers, thought Fina, then I imagine you can. But she kept quiet.

"Cyril Lighton's issue is still the same as before – the named professorship he so desperately wanted. Let's turn to the family," continued Ruby.

"I think you forgot Ian," said Fina in a quiet voice, knowing it was a sore spot.

"Ian, yes. How could I forget," said Ruby with a sardonic smile. "Well, I cannot see how Leslie's death changes anything for him – can you?"

"No, you're right. Let's move on to the family now, as you suggested. I don't know why they would have a reason to wish

Leslie out of the way, either. Though there could be something about that locket that we don't know about."

"Yes... that locket. I hope Charles has some information about that. Speaking of Charles, I assume we can rule him out, as well as the rest of the staff?" said Ruby with a distinct twinkle in her eye.

Fina tried to appear nonchalant about the suggestion. It was no good, though, as she could feel the heat rising in her cheeks. "I cannot see a motive for Charles, nor the rest of the staff."

"No, you're right. There could be something, but we just don't know. If Granville had survived and come into his inheritance, then the entire house could be upended or even sold, and everyone could lose their jobs. Hardly a reason to risk hanging, though," said Ruby. Her eyes widened in embarrassment over her faux pas. "I'm sorry – I did it again, Fina."

"It's perfectly natural under the circumstances," said Fina in a steady voice, though her lips quivered. "The staff are out of it as far as I can see."

Ruby sighed. "This feels hopeless until we can work out where everyone was and what they were doing when the deaths occurred. Nearly everyone has at least one motive, if not more. Including ourselves."

A rather dismal silence was interrupted by the entrance of Charles with the tea and toast. "I asked Mary and the cook about their whereabouts today," said Charles as he set the tray down carefully on the bed.

"And?" asked Ruby.

"And they said they were in the scullery all day, cleaning and preparing meals. I suppose they could be in on it together," he said with a wink in Fina's direction.

"Very funny, Charles," said Fina, eyeing the toast and tea hungrily.

Ruby did not seem to see the humour in the situation. "What about yourself – and Grimston?"

"Old Grimston could have bumped off Leslie, but he has an alibi for the first murder, just like me." Picking up on the seriousness of Ruby's tone, Fina wondered whether Charles was being perhaps a touch too flippant about his whereabouts. No, she thought, I can trust Charles. Yes.

"Are you alright, Fina?" asked Charles with sudden concern. "You looked so far away – I'm worried about your head."

"Oh no, Charles. Thank you. Just thinking."

"Well, I'd better be on my way if I don't want a thorough tongue lashing from Mrs Lynn or Grimston."

After the door closed, Fina began to munch away happily, enjoying the slightly sinful feeling of eating toast in bed in the early evening. "Mmm... want a slice, Ruby? It's marvellously satisfying," she said as she sipped the strong milky tea.

"Don't mind if I do," she said, swiping a piece and slathering it with marmalade. "It is scrumptious. I feel almost ready to face the hordes downstairs."

"How in heaven's name are we going to get them all to tell us where they were when the second murder was committed? We cannot just ask them individually and expect them to confess. We have the same problem with the initial C from that bloody – sorry – locket. If someone has a middle name that begins with C they're unlikely to reveal it. We have to devise some sort of plan for tonight," said Fina, stopping this rant long enough to look up at the window. She sighed and continued. "Time is not on our side. The snow will stop at some point and the inevitable march of the police will begin."

"Feens, we have to keep our wits about us. The only way to find out about the middle names of our guests is to search their rooms for identification papers of some sort—"

"—and look for the poison! I imagine, though, that the murderer disposed of the poison already," said Fina, dejectedly.

"Not necessarily. Remember, we could have – and did – make that assumption with the first murder. But the murderer held onto it in case they needed it again. It turns out that they did – since we're operating on the assumption of one murderer."

They both sat silent for a few moments, sipping tea and staring into the crackling fire. A light tap came at the door. Ruby rose and let in Charles.

"Grimston has things well in hand, so I have a bit of extra time. What schemes have you two cooked up for this evening?" he said with a grin.

"We were just discussing two tasks for this evening. One is to search the guest rooms. The second is to find out everyone's movements for the first murder, since we cannot do that effectively for the second."

He nodded. "What about a re-enactment?"

"Re-enactment?" said Ruby, her hands flying up in excitement. "That's a brilliant idea, Charles." She went over to him and gave him an emphatic kiss on the cheek, disregarding the bright lipstick print left on his cheek. She continued, "Yes, that's exactly what we'll have to do. How will we convince everyone to go along with it, though?"

"If we can convince the Countess to agree to make the suggestion, I'm sure the other guests wouldn't dare to decline," said Fina with a smile.

"Perfect. Charles, do you think she'll agree if you say it was our suggestion?" asked Ruby.

"I don't see why not. We get on well. And she seems to have respect for the two of you. Strangely enough, she has a soft spot for women who work. I think she finds it rather romantic," said Charles. He got up slowly to go on his errand.

Ruby drew out a handkerchief from her dress pocket and gently wiped Charles' now-red-with-embarrassment cheek.

"Wait a minute, Charles," said Fina. "We'll need you to search the rooms for the poison and identification papers that will tell us if anyone has a name beginning with C. You're the only one who can do it. If Ruby or I were to be caught... well, you've already seen what happened to me," she said, rubbing the back of her head. "Whereas you can find some legitimate excuse."

"I agree, but the only fly in the ointment is that we need Charles to be there for the re-enactment," said Ruby.

"That's not a problem," said Charles. "You see, Grimston and I were together – for the exception of a minute or two, here and there – for the entire evening. We would have seen the same people coming and going. I will be sure to speak to him before the re-enactment to tell him my memories. He's a sharp old bird."

"Spiffing," said Fina. "We'll send you on your way, Charles. We'll get dressed for cocktails, assuming your tête-à-tête with the Countess is successful."

26

An hour later, everyone had assembled in the drawing room. It was remarkably similar to the first evening – with some notable absences, of course, thought Fina. With Ruby's assistance, Fina had dressed in her favourite tea gown. Fina felt her mother would be proud of her dressing her best even when she felt at her worst.

The Countess, in the most officious tone she could summon, called everyone to attention. She had girded herself for the part in the uncharacteristic armour of an onyx lace dress, complete with a rather Edwardian high collar. In return, the guests gifted her their rapt attention.

"Dearest guests. I know the past few days have been most unorthodox. I have lost a dear nephew and we just learned about Mr Dashwood's expiration. This cannot go on," she said, as if they were a group of small children who had been behaving badly.

"Therefore," she continued, her voice gaining strength and volume. "I have asked us all here in the drawing room so that we might recreate our exact movements on the night of my dear nephew's death."

Gasp.

"Dearest Auntie, do you think that wise?" asked Charlotte, as if she were handling a delicate piece of china.

Cyril, looking more pleased with himself than usual – which was quite a feat, thought Fina – also stepped forward. "Hear, hear, Lady Charlotte. I agree."

"I jolly well disagree with you," said Edgar in a strong, steady voice. He looked remarkably less sozzled, despite his lunchtime performance. "We need to get to the bottom of this mess. We could pass off my brother's death as an accident, but two deaths? Not bloody well likely."

"Edgar!" exclaimed the Countess.

Edgar sat calmly, ignoring his aunt. Fina noticed he had temporarily relinquished his usual habit of scraping skin from his thumbs.

"I am willing to try a re-enactment, but what makes the movements of the earlier evening so special? Wasn't Granville poisoned later in the evening?" Ian rejoined.

Ruby proceeded to explain the nature of the poisoning and why they had to account for their movements early on. Ian seemed mollified. Or at least he didn't want to contradict Ruby, thought Fina.

"Right. Let us push on, shall we?" said the Earl, rubbing his hands. "Grimston, you keep the time," nodding in his direction.

"Very good, sir," Grimston replied.

Ever the ham, the Earl warmed to his role as director. "Now then, what came first?"

Gayatri responded, "We had a spill of candle wax on my dress. Then Miss Dove made her offer of the stain remover."

"Right – and everyone heard that, correct?" said the Earl, swivelling his head around the room to make sure he received affirmations from everyone. "Does anyone remember what time this occurred?"

Gayatri said, "It was at 6:45 – or very near that time. I know because I was standing near Sajida and the fireplace. When the candle spilled on my dress, she put the candle back and I noted the time because of the clock on the mantelpiece."

"Splendid. Yes. Now, Miss Badarur and Miss Dove, will you retrace your footsteps and actions precisely?" the Earl requested, motioning to Gayatri and Ruby. Giving affirmation by their departure, the Earl rumbled on. "Now, Grimston, you ring the gong for dinner at the precise time you did on that evening."

"It will be my pleasure, milord," said Grimston, bowing and leaving the room.

"Shall we all mingle while we wait?" asked the Countess in a jovial manner. Though the joviality was forced, Fina appreciated her effort.

Everyone had paired off again, as they had that first night. Cyril and Edgar, Julia and Ian, the Earl and Countess, Sajida and Gayatri – though Sajida was alone as Gayatri and Ruby had played their part in the re-enactment by exiting the room. Granville and Leslie. Only Charlotte remained. Fina felt it was significant, somehow, but she couldn't put her finger on why, exactly. Did it mean something that Charlotte was alone? She and Sajida had found one another to talk to, so Fina stepped over to join them at the fireplace. Perhaps talking to Charlotte would help shake loose whatever was lodged in the back of her mind.

Charlotte was all smiles, but they were painted-on smiles. Small wonder given that her brother had just been murdered. Fina wondered how she really felt about that. They had seemed so distant as brother and sister. She wanted to ask about it, but knew it wasn't the time. She looked at Sajida. Though she was an expert at make-up, she could still see traces of circles under her eyes. Charlotte and Sajida were nattering away about their trips abroad, though their excessive nodding seemed to indicate their minds were elsewhere. Fina also nodded appreciatively, but was distracted by her musings.

She glanced again around the room, sizing up everyone's body language. Cyril and Edgar had moved into a recess in the corner. Their shoulders were rigid. Definitely an air of conspiracy about their conversation.

The Earl and Countess sat in two chairs near the fire, not facing one another directly. Their conversation was sporadic and staccato, like that of the long-married couple they had been.

Ian and Julia were ensconced by the cabinet with curios, leaning against it casually. Their shoulders slumped, though it was not through resignation. They looked genuinely relaxed.

The gong sounded from the hallway.

27

As they all entered the dining room, Ruby and Gayatri came in from the hall, just as they had that first evening. While they all filed in – almost in a military formation – Edgar stopped. He said, "I say, Ian, I–I–I don't remember you walking in with us. I believe you joined us later in the dining room, what?"

"Yes, that's right, Edgar," replied Cyril. "Dashed odd that you're not re-enacting *your* part, Mr Clavering."

Ian's body stiffened, but his face remained impassive. "Forgive me, I did not recall that, but you're absolutely correct. I did need to attend to – a call of nature." He marched off in the direction of the lavatory.

The Earl motioned to Grimston, "Grimston, make sure you note the time Mr Clavering returns."

"I will endeavour to do so, sir," he replied, pulling out a tiny notebook from this pocket.

Fina was making note of the time herself. By the time Ian had returned to the dining room, precisely sixteen minutes had elapsed. Everyone agreed that it seemed like the correct time as the soup was just being served. Just barely enough time to carry out the murder – though he would need to move like lightning.

Fina did consider him a weak candidate, however. He had been hoping to winkle some funds out of Granville, so he was hardly likely to kill the goose that laid the golden eggs. And the chances of a guest – rather than a member of the family – knowing the precise location of Ruby and Granville's rooms seemed unlikely.

"Excuse me, Ian," said Fina over her soup. "Is this your first time to Pauncefort Hall?"

He eyed her suspiciously. "Why do you want to know?"

She decided honesty was the best way to get an answer. In fact, it was the only avenue open to her because she couldn't think up anything other than a flimsy retort. "If you were the murderer—"

"But I'm not," he said firmly, nearly dropping his spoon in the soup.

"Of course, I'm not saying that you *are* the murderer. I just want to clear something up that I thought of while you were... away. It seems to me that if you had not visited Pauncefort before, it would be unlikely that you would know the location of Granville's bedroom, much less Ruby's bedroom. Therefore, it would be difficult for you to complete the necessary steps in just sixteen minutes if you didn't know the lay of the land."

He leaned back in his chair and dabbed his mouth with a napkin, delicately. "You're right, of course. The answer to your question is no, I haven't visited Pauncefort Hall before."

"Well that settles it," said Fina.

"Unfortunately, honesty compels me to say, however, that I did know the location of both rooms. Grimston pointed out Granville's when I first arrived. As for Ruby, I saw her leaving her room, by chance, on the way down to drinks that night," he said. "So that means I am still in the so-called running. Though I can assure you, I did not do it."

Ian signalled that the interrogation was over by turning to talk to the Countess on his right.

Feeling restless, Fina turned to Charlotte on her left. They had exhausted the topics of clothes, fashion and Oxford. She thought she'd try her hand at learning more about the family history. "Do you live at Pauncefort most of the year, Charlotte – with your aunt and uncle?"

"Yes, I have lived here all my life. My aunt and uncle came to live with us after my mother died. I was only five years old then, so they're practically my second parents. We get on together quite well," she said, with a fond smile in their direction.

"They seem like a lovely couple," said Fina, hoping to soften the blow of her next question. "I know this is a difficult time to ask, but did your mother die in some sort of accident or was she ill for quite some time?"

Charlotte eyed her warily. "Well, as I was an infant at the time, I only know the story second-hand. The family tale is that she died of a broken heart. At least that's what the family told me when I was a child. That year was a difficult year. My uncle – the Earl – fell ill. Granville was headed to boarding school and apparently he was quite upset about it. There was some sort of business trouble that my father had to attend to in St Kitts. My mother gave birth to her fourth child, but it was stillborn. From what Granville told me, she was physically strong at first, but then, quite suddenly, died. Everyone assumed that it was because she had lost the will to live."

"You sound like you don't quite believe that yourself – do you have another theory about her death?" asked Fina. Her mind raced. This wasn't the story they had heard from the cook! Did the family just want to protect the children from the truth?

Charlotte shifted in her seat, smoothing her skirt. "Oh, does it sound that way? No – though I don't think she literally died of a broken heart, it is plausible that she was weak and had lost the will to live."

Fina was distracted by Grimston materializing out of thin air, and whispering something into the Earl's ear. The Earl cleared his throat and said, "Ahem. My friends, Grimston informs me that it is time for the ladies to move to the library for coffee. We will reconvene in the saloon at nine."

Trickling out of the dining room – just as they had that first night, the Countess lifted her skirts and made a dramatic exit. In case it hadn't been made abundantly clear already, she made a waving motion at Grimston to signal her departure.

Fina was the last to leave. A light tap on her shoulder made her spin round. Charles whispered, "I've found out quite a bit about all of our friends – including you two," he said with a face that was somewhere between angry and disappointed.

"You searched our rooms?" hissed Fina. "How dare you!" she said, trying to control the volume of her voice. Only Julia looked back and seemed to notice their intense conversation. "We mustn't talk now or we'll miss the rest of the re-enactment. You'd better go find Grimston," she said in a commanding tone.

"I'm following you – there's no one else to keep track of the ladies in the library. And after what I found out, I definitely want to keep an eye on all of you," he said in a low growl.

Stomping off into the library, Fina flounced down on the couch like a small child.

Charlotte rose to leave almost as soon as her aunt entered the room. Charles made note of her departure in a small note-book. He stood sentry near the door.

Conversation was desultory and disjointed among the women. Everyone looked simultaneously bored and nervous, thought Fina. After what seemed to be an interminable time discussing the decline of modern standards of all sorts, Charles signalled that it was time to make an excursion to the saloon.

Ruby whispered to Fina, "You should pretend you have a headache and need to go to bed. Tell Charles to meet you so he can tell you what he found. Make sure you lock your door so the person who was tempted to cosh you on the head won't be able to succeed again. I'll keep watch on what happens down here."

Fina opened her mouth to say that Charles had most certainly found something – something about them – but it was too late. She had been carried along with the wave of the crowd into the saloon.

28

Despite the warmth of the fire, Fina shivered in front of the fireplace in her room. *Mustn't be so hard on myself.* After all, she thought as she lightly touched the back of her head, she had just been nearly murdered! Where *was* that box of chocolates? She could really accommodate an entire box of chocolates in her stomach right now. She tiptoed into Ruby's room and spied the white box with red trim sitting on the bed. Scooping it up, she half ran, half tiptoed back to her room.

"Hello," said Charles. Fina nearly tripped over the chair nearest the door.

Holding a hand over her chest, she said, "How did you get in here? You gave me the most terrible fright."

"You forget, I work here. That means I have the keys to all of the rooms," he said with a devious grin.

For a moment, Fina's heart leapt into her mouth. Was his smile a conspiratorial grin or a threatening one? Had she been too trusting? Her mother always told her she was too trusting of human nature. *Yes, but this was Charles...*

His languid, casual movement to the chair by the fire told her that it was all in her mind.

"Now," she said. "Let's get down to business. What's all this tripe about finding out something about us?" If she started with an accusation, she might get the upper hand.

No such luck. Charles' smile remained, but his tone was cool. "I found the papers – about Granville and some place called 'Bluegate' – wedged between the mattress and the bed frame in Ruby's room. I don't know what it means, exactly, but I believe it gives her – and possibly you – a motive for the murders. I'm not going to tell you anything else until you come clean."

"Come clean?" mocked Fina. "What is this, an American film?" She was playing for time. What had the papers been doing under Ruby's mattress? Surely she had handed them over to Gayatri and Sajida earlier that morning. Or at least, that's what she had said. Hadn't she?

Rising and pacing around the room for a moment, she came back to sit on the bed, shoulders bent in a conspiratorial manner toward Charles' chair. "Promise not to tell anyone. And I mean anyone. Including the police," she said.

"You know I can't do that. Especially since this is a murder enquiry. I'm fair at keeping a low profile and at keeping secrets, but I've never been interrogated. I might crack."

Fina winced at the imagery. "No one is going to give you the third degree, Charles."

"Now who's quoting American films? How do you know? Besides, I'm a member of the staff. They go easy on toffs like you."

"Toffs like – forget it. You're right. I have to tell you, but you do need to know that the consequences of you 'cracking' as you call it could mean that either Ruby or I could go to the gallows."

"Cripes."

"Exactly." Taking his expletive as a sign of agreement, Fina proceeded to tell Charles – in as vague terms as possible – why they were at Pauncefort Hall that weekend. Charles' eyes grew larger and larger.

"Well that's a pretty pickle, Fina. But in some sort of half-cocked way it makes sense. I wondered why the two of you would want to come to a place like this," he said, leaning back in a more relaxed position. "You may be dressmakers, but you both seemed interested in more than just frills and furbelows."

Fina muttered, "Ruby is going to kill me." Charles stared at her, willing her to realize the import of her words. "I–I mean, you know what I mean." She held her head in her hands. "What are we to do?"

Charles reached across and gently touched her hand. "I think what I've found in those rooms should help us solve this case, so let's save the worrying until later."

Lips pursed, Fina nodded. Straightening up, she said "What did you find? Let's start with their names. Who has an initial C?"

"Well, besides what we already discussed – Lady Charlotte and the Countess' names, Julia's is Cicely. So that means that Gayatri, Sajida, you, Miss Ruby and the men are out of the running, assuming it implicates a woman because of the necklace. It doesn't mean they are or aren't the murderer, but it is useful information," he said.

"Yes," Fina agreed. "I think it would do to press them further – maybe show them the locket?"

"Perhaps, though I'd be worried it might provoke the murderer again," said Charles.

"It's a risk we may have to take, though. Time is running short. What about the poison and any other items of interest you found in the rooms? The suspense is frightfully difficult to take."

"Well..." said Charles, pausing with a grin.

"Go on!" said Fina, grinning back.

Ruby burst into the room, cutting off any further discussion.

Her perfectly coiffed hair was dishevelled from running up the stairs.

"Come quickly – there's been an accident!"

29

Everyone sat in chairs in a single-file line across the saloon. Fina thought they looked like a group of anxious schoolchildren waiting to see the headmaster for their naughty behaviour.

Edgar was sitting – lying, rather – on a settee, apart, with his legs up on a chair. He pressed a handkerchief to the back of his head, as if he were pushing himself to rise from the sofa. Fina could see that there were slashes of blood laid starkly against the cream of the material and that sandy, greasy hair. Gayatri sat next to him, examining the back of his head.

"What happened?" said Fina, rushing to Gayatri.

"I'm afraid, sweetie, someone coshed him on the head," said Julia. "Just like you."

After taking a long drag on her cigarette, Julia nodded her head in the direction of the Earl, who looked to be a particularly pale shade of green, rather than his standard red. "The Earl found him lying in the hallway – as a part of our jolly recreation of the crime."

The Earl winced and shook his head. "Ghastly business. I just cannot think what's happening to our home. Edgar was sprawled face down on the tiles."

Charles coughed politely. "May I enquire, milord, who was absent during this time?"

Grimston stepped forward, holding his small notepad at arm's length, peering imperiously over his small, wire-rimmed spectacles.

"At 9:24, Professor Lighton exited the saloon.

At 9:26, Master Edgar exited.

At 9:32, Lady Charlotte exited.

At 9:34, Professor Lighton returned.

At 9:36, Lord Snittlegarth exited.

At 9:40, Miss Aston exited.

At 9:42, Lady Charlotte returned.

At 9:45, Lord Snittlegarth returned as he had just found Master Edgar in the hallway near the men's... ahem..."

"Yes, yes, Grimston, we know exactly what you mean. My God, is this place Victoria Station?" asked the Earl. "Did we all really make this many entrances and exits that evening, Grimston?"

"I'm afraid so, milord," said Grimston, impassively.

"How the deuce did Cyril, Charlotte and Julia all miss Edgar lying in the hallway?" asked Ian with exasperation in his voice. He gripped his brandy snifter so tight Fina was afraid it might shatter. Ruby looked over at Fina with a look of horror – apparently at Ian's near loss of control.

Turning to the Earl, Ruby asked, "Would the only people likely to see Edgar lying on the floor be men – since he was found near the lavatory?"

He scratched the back of his balding head. "I suppose so, Miss Dove. He was far enough down the hallway near the main corridor that you wouldn't notice unless you turned to look that way when returning to the saloon. Yes, I'd say a man could not have failed to notice – a woman might have seen him, but not necessarily."

All eyes turned to Cyril. He shrank visibly into his chair, his face quickly becoming the colour of his starched shirt. "What are you all looking at? I didn't see Edgar lying on the floor. I passed him in the hallway on my return to the saloon. He was going in the opposite direction, so I assume he was going to the same place I had been." He stood up suddenly, wrapping his hands on the arms of his chair. "You can't pin this on me! I like Edgar. He has been one of my best students."

The Countess, who was sitting in the chair next to Cyril, touched him lightly on the arm. "No one is accusing you, Professor Lighton," she said in a calm voice, though she began to twist her wedding ring again. "There's obviously some madman hiding in Pauncefort Hall. He must have slipped in before the storm and been ferreting about, poisoning my loved ones and battering others on the head." She said this sentence as much to herself as to the rest of the room.

Fina wondered if she should argue out loud with this fairy tale. Or perhaps it could somehow serve their sleuthing purposes? After all, if the killer were lulled into a false sense of security...

Ruby cleared her throat. "Perhaps we should look at this in a slightly different manner. It is true that only a man would have seen the aftermath of the attack, but that does not mean that a woman couldn't have attacked Edgar. If what Cyril says is true – that he saw Edgar going to the lavatory – then Edgar could have been attacked when he went down the hallway from behind by Lady Charlotte or Julia. I know this is unpleasant, but that is what might have happened."

Ian said, obviously rising to Julia's defence, "Well, what's to say that Edgar didn't bash in his own head? To make it look like he had been attacked."

"Why would he do that?" asked Sajida.

"To divert suspicion away from himself," said Fina, looking toward Gayatri for confirmation of her theory.

Gayatri shook her head. "No, it's not possible that he did this to himself. It's at the wrong angle," she said, pointing at the wound as if to demonstrate.

"I say," said Cyril. "Where's the weapon? Did you see it in the hallway, Grimston?"

"Yes, sir. I put it in a small cupboard near the saloon for safe-keeping. It was a candlestick that I recognized from the library. It was decidedly the weapon, as it bore traces of the mishap you see on Master Edgar's scalp."

"From the library. So anyone could have taken it?"

Grimston cleared his throat. "Yes, sir. Any one of those present here tonight."

30

Silence descended on the room. Fina swore she could hear the snowflakes falling on the French windows at the opposite end of the saloon. No one wants to discuss this further, she thought. The possibilities are too uncomfortable. She thought she might change tack for a moment.

"Grimston, what is the result of our re-enactment thus far? Who had enough time to plant the poison?" she asked. Strangely, everyone looked relieved to be discussing a larger pool of suspects, Fina thought.

Flipping through the pages of his notebook with deft precision, the faithful retainer began to read. The monotone voice sounded like he was reviewing the daily menu with the cook. "The guests who had time enough – according to the estimates provided earlier – were the following, in rank order: Mr Clavering, Lady Snittlegarth, Professor Lighton, Lady Charlotte, Miss Aston, Miss Gayatri Badarur, Miss Aubrey-Havelock, Miss Sajida Badarur, Miss Dove and Lord Snittlegarth. From my discussions with Charles, we've ascertained that Master Granville had time as well during the evening. Master Edgar may or may not have had enough time as well, but the timing was – ahem – delayed by the assault he suffered in the hallway."

"But, but, but, Grimston, that is absolutely everyone!" spluttered the Earl.

"I am reluctant to say so, yes, milord," said Grimston gravely.

Turning to his wife, the Earl said emphatically. "I am afraid your theory about the madman must be true, m'dear. It's the only one that makes any sense."

"With all due respect, Lord Snittlegarth, where is this madman hiding, and why in heaven's name would he do such a thing?" asked Cyril.

"There's pots of rooms here, and as for the reason... well... does a madman need a reason?" said the Earl.

"Lord Snittlegarth, it's true there's pots of room at Pauncefort, but it's hardly likely he could go undetected this entire weekend," responded Julia.

Slapping his legs and rising, Ian said, "I say we form a search party to look for this supposed madman. What else are we to do? Sit here and wonder about one another?"

This caused quite a stir among the guests. Everyone started talking at once. It was clear that no one agreed with one another about the wisdom of moving forward with such an idea, thought Fina.

Moving his hands as if he were banging on a grand piano, Ian motioned to them all to calm down. "As the Countess had the original theory about a madman, why don't we let her decide?"

Looking slightly perturbed that she needed one of her guests to guide the party, the Countess spoke. "The advisability of such an action is questionable, particularly given what has now happened to my nephew."

Edgar nodded almost imperceptibly from the settee, Fina noticed.

Holding up her hand as if she were directing traffic, the Countess continued. "However, given the direness of this situation, I see no other alternative. I suggest we form parties of three and search each floor of the house."

Everyone looked at one another. Ian took the initiative. "Fine. I'll search with Julia and Ruby," looking at them for agreement. After they nodded their heads, the Countess said, "I will not join the search, but I will stay here to tend to Edgar."

Fina said, "I'll search with Charles and Gayatri." Sajida continued the round robin. "I guess that leaves Cyril, Charlotte, Lord Snittlegarth and myself, correct?"

"Yes, that rounds it off nicely. Grimston will stay here in case we need something to be fetched," said the Countess. Grimston registered agreement by merely pursing his lips.

"What do we do if we find this mysterious madman? Clap him in irons?" asked Julia, waving away the smoke from her cigarette. "I may be quite talented at playing a role, but I'm not talented at taking down a gimlet-eyed lunatic."

Heads nodded in agreement around the room. There was a heavy silence until the Earl spoke in grave tones. "Yes, yes, m'dear. Quite right, quite right. If you find this dangerous individual, don't try to do anything, other than perhaps lock him in a room. I doubt even that would be possible, but it would be ideal. No, the best plan of action is to return to us and report his location." Straightening himself up like a general, he intoned, "Then I'll confront the miscreant myself."

The saloon gradually emptied. "What utter rot," said Fina when she had joined Charles and Gayatri as members of her search party. "We all know one of us committed these murders – as well as the attacks on Edgar and Fina."

"True," said Gayatri. "But we'd better go through with it so we have something to report. Besides, it will keep our minds occupied. I don't know about you, but I'm feeling rather on edge," she said. Fina watched as Gayatri slipped off her silver heels – presumably so they wouldn't alert the purported madman during their search.

Fina and Charles followed Gayatri's lead. Now in stockings, they tiptoed up the stairs to the first floor landing. Fina's feet sank into the deep carpets that lined the floor. She felt freed – almost excited. Though her toes were a bit cold. In room after room, they searched, to no avail.

As they were making their way into the final bathroom, they heard a piercing scream – a high-pitched voice – coming from the second floor. They dashed up the stairs to find Charlotte, crying uncontrollably. The Earl had enveloped her in an embrace in an attempt to comfort her. "I–I–I saw, I saw him!" she exclaimed.

"Where?" asked Fina.

"In the corridor," said Charlotte, her eyes darting from side to side, reminding Fina of the windscreen wipers on the car in which they arrived to this cursed weekend. "As we were entering this room. I was the last one to file in, and out of the corner of my eye I saw movement and a flash. A flash of green – a green coat."

"Are you quite sure?" asked Cyril. "Perhaps it's just mental strain," he said in his most imperious Oxford Don tones.

"Please don't patronize me, Professor Lighton," said Charlotte, pushing her hair back from her forehead and wiping away her tears with the Earl's handkerchief. "I know you're trying to be helpful, but I saw what I saw," she said firmly. "There's someone hiding – no, lurking – at Pauncefort Hall."

31

Everyone huddled around the persistently cheerful fire in the drawing room. Quite the picturesque Yuletide scene, thought Fina, sourly. Blankets covered their legs and brandy snifters were close at hand. Edgar was now erect, on a sofa near the fire. He, Grimston and the Countess had been informed about the sighting of 'the green man' – as he had been christened given his sartorial choices.

The Earl cleared his throat. "Now that we have confirmed that there is, indeed, a madman at Pauncefort, I suggest that we all stay alert and remain – at the very least – in pairs. When you retire for the evening," he said looking up at the mantel clock that now read midnight, "Please be sure to lock your doors. It's possible that this ah, green man has a key, so I suggest you lock yourself in, as it were."

This seemed to be the signal for the party – if you could call it that now, thought Fina – to break up. Everyone did leave in pairs to climb the stairs to their bedrooms. Charles, Ruby and Fina remained.

Peering out of the window, Fina noticed the snow had stopped. The moon was obscured by a few clouds, but the reflection on the snow gave it an eerie blue sparkle. Peaceful. Quiet. Too quiet.

Glancing over at Charles and Ruby, she noticed their haggard faces for the first time. Ruby's shoulders tensed up, giving the appearance of a shortened neck. Charles slumped on the chair as if he had surrendered to whatever inevitable nightmare was to come. Fina was sure she looked a sight herself. She noticed a slight trembling in her left hand.

Fina decided that honesty was the best policy with Charles. "I'd like to speak to Ruby – alone – for a few minutes, if you please, Charles. My nerves are shot and I think the best thing for me would be a warm cup of cocoa. Could you make us all some cocoa? We could come with you if you're worried about being alone, though."

"No, no..." he said, his masculinity clearly affronted. "Besides, Grimston should be somewhere about in one of the ground floor rooms. I'll take him with me." Fina noticed his upper lip was trembling ever so slightly. She found it endearing.

He padded out of the room, slowly and with precision. It must be because he's worried about making a noise on the tiles, thought Fina.

She sat on a sofa facing Ruby and, folding her feet comfortably underneath her, she let out a great sigh of relief, though relief was hardly the emotion coursing through her veins.

"What did you learn from Charles? What did he find during the search?" asked Ruby.

There was a long, awkward pause. Finally Fina spoke. "I–I haven't heard the full report from Charles yet."

"Why ever not? He had plenty of time to debrief you! Oh, let me guess..." she said with a wink and a smile, her shoulders relaxing a little.

As always, Fina felt the heat rise in her cheeks. "Of course not! Besides, I'm injured. No, I really do wish that were the actual reason for why we didn't finish discussing all of the details. No, I'm afraid..." she stammered, staring into the fire instead of looking at Ruby. "I'm afraid that Charles found the Bluegate papers underneath your mattress."

Fina had read about the expression 'jaw dropping' in literature, but had always thought it to be a bit of a descriptive exaggeration. Ruby's face proved her wrong. She slumped back into the sofa as if Fina had risen to push her back.

"I'm so sorry," said Fina.

"No, don't judge yourself. I should have thought of that possibility. I suppose the only way to have avoided that would have been to stay in my room. Or for me to hide them in your room while he searched. I've been so focused on the murders that I completely forgot about it."

"It took me by surprise, I must admit. I thought you told me this morning you'd handed over the papers already."

Ruby stared. "Handed them over? To whom?"

Fina shifted her position on the sofa. That morning seemed so long ago. She had sensed the importance of keeping quiet then, but now, with two bodies on their hands, it was time to speak openly. "To Gayatri, of course. Or Sajida. Our contacts?"

"Gayatri!" Ruby's voice could hardly sound more astonished. "Why, Fina, darling, she's nothing to do with the Bluegate papers. Nor is Sajida. You've got the wrong end of the stick. I was asked to bring them back to Oxford."

It was Fina's turn to stare. "So they're not involved, after all?"

"Not that I know of. Although it was an excellent piece of deduction on your part," Ruby said kindly. She sighed. "I suppose you explained to Charles what it meant?"

"I had to, but I was as vague as possible. He didn't seem upset by it. Actually, I was more upset with him for searching your room than he was about the reason for searching. Although I don't think he fully grasps the politics of it, I do think he would be sympathetic – if the circumstances were right to explain it. I think we're all so focused on the murders that little else seems important at this point."

Ruby nodded, though she had covered her eyes with her hands – a sure sign of an incipient headache, thought Fina.

Hoping to distract her – even if it was with another distressing subject, Fina asked, "What's your theory about the murders at this point?"

"Honestly, rather than think about most likely suspects, I'm working on elimination. Who couldn't have done it?"

"Well, Gayatri and you – unless you two conspired – are out of the running because you didn't exit during the evening except to remove the stain from her dress. It also seems that Edgar and I are out of the running, since this 'green man' person coshed us both," Fina said, wincing as her fingers brushed the back of her head.

32

Charles carried a tray into the room with three cups of piping hot cocoa. Fina felt absurdly pleased seeing the steam rising from the cups. The mixture was perfect – just enough milk – not enough to overpower the taste of the chocolate.

Feeling revived, she turned to Charles. "I told Ruby about what you found in her room." Charles stared into the fire. Fina put a hand on his shoulder. "You did as we asked. And now you know. But you know we're not the murderers."

Charles sighed. "Apparently everyone has secrets at Pauncefort Hall."

A light flashed in Ruby's eyes. "That must include you, Charles. It's only sporting that you share your secret with us. You seem much too competent to be working here in this capacity. Not that you don't do your job admirably – it's just that it seems you might be cut out for something more challenging."

Charles smiled at the compliment. Fina could see he wasn't fooled by the pointed question disguised under flattery, however.

"You two are quite the detectives, aren't you? Well, yes, I suppose it is only sporting – as you say." He made himself comfortable in a chair by the fire, looking for all the world as though he was about to settle down with a storybook, thought Fina.

"My mother died when I was quite young. None of the family knew what happened to my father – much less anything about him. My mother died in disgrace because I was illegitimate, as they say. She had been disowned by the family when she found herself in trouble. The family urged her, apparently, to give me up for adoption. It was fortunate that she didn't because who knows what would have become of me. My aunt and uncle took me in. They provided for me in every way – posh schools, well-fed and well-clothed. But, as happens so often with toffs that have enormous amounts of money, they give you everything but love and affection. Though I am to blame for what followed, I also know that I felt desperate about not really being wanted, I suppose."

Charles' eyes began to well up. Clenching his jaw, he continued. "In any case, I left home and fell in with what I suppose would be called a 'bad lot'. Drugs, petty theft, drinking – the usual. One day, we planned something spectacular – at least for us. A jewel robbery. It all went pear-shaped, and I was left – literally – holding the bag of stolen emeralds. I took the fall for it and went to prison for three years. When I got out, I wanted to go to university. I was accepted to Oxford, but when they found out about my time in prison, they withdrew the offer – just a week before the term started. So I went into service. One day, this position at Pauncefort Hall turned up and I applied. I've been here almost ten months now. And I'm grateful for the job."

"What you say rings true, Charles, but I can't help but think there's more. Why here? Why now?" said Ruby, in a kind but firm voice.

"Ah, I forget that you two are not only amateur detectives, but you're actually, ah, spies, aren't you?" he said with a sardonic grin. "You always know there's more beneath – even with my convincing and true story."

Hunching over his shoulders, he stared at the rug and continued. "Yes, the judge who sent me down was Justice Henry Sykes-Duckworth, also known as the Earl of Malvern and father of Charlotte, Edgar and Granville. That was before he decided to spend nearly all his time in the Caribbean, so he could concentrate on swelling his own coffers, blast him!"

He took a deep breath and carried on. "I know you're thinking that it's too much of a coincidence that I started working here. And you're right. When I saw the position open up, I jumped at the opportunity, thinking that I would get my revenge, somehow – after all, he does come home once a year or so. I had no idea what I would do, though, or how. Once I took the position I was surprised to find that it suited my temperament. I was content. I also had let go of a lot of my anger, believe it or not! At any rate, if I were to want to murder someone, it would be Henry Sykes-Duckworth, not his son."

"You could have thought it would be better revenge than killing him directly – make him live through the suffering of a loss of a child," responded Ruby.

"Yes, I see your point, except for one thing. Granville and his father were not close. From the staff gossip, I've gathered that the two of them never got on well. Even when he was a child. Apparently it all became much worse once Granville's mother, Catherine, died suddenly. But they had already been on that path for a while. No, if I had wanted to hurt him through hurting his kin, I would have targeted Charlotte or Edgar. Both of them dote on their father and he feels quite close to them. I have to admit that I've become fond of them as well."

"Thank you, Charles, for being honest with us," said Fina as he looked up from the fascinating rug. "Now that we have cleared that up, let us move on to what you found after your search – other than the Bluegate papers, of course."

"Disappointingly little, as it happens. The Badarur sisters had some letters from their mother, but they were mostly just family gossip." He said the words lightly, but with an air of suppressed excitement, as if there was more to come.

Ruby cocked her head inquisitively. "What about the poison?" she asked. "Could you find traces of it anywhere?"

"Oh yes," he said with a slow smile.

"Go on," said Ruby.

"Tell us, you miscreant, as the Earl would say," Fina said, crouching down as if it could increase her sense of hearing.

"It was in the back of Julia Aston's wardrobe."

Fina choked on her cocoa.

"Interesting," was Ruby's only reply.

"Interesting?" said Fina, somewhat desperately. "Is that all you can say? She must be the murderer! She had every chance to do it – and she must have hated him much more strongly than she let on."

"Perhaps," said Ruby, apparently lost in thought.

Charles eyes grew wide as he sat back in disbelief. "You don't seem to think it important, Ruby. Why not? Julia must be the murderer."

Out of the corner of her eye, Fina saw a shadow lurking. Whipping her head around, she saw it was Grimston.

"Ladies," he said, bowing in a calm voice. "Charles, please make haste. There has been an unfortunate occurrence upstairs."

33

On the landing outside of the Countess' bedroom, Fina spied Grimston, Charles, and the Earl and Countess, huddled in a tight circle. The circle parted to swallow up Fina and Ruby as they approached.

"By the number of times you pulled your bell pull, I ascertained this summons was of an urgent nature," said Grimston, breathless, but in his still-perfectly-level voice.

Waving the aubergine-coloured sleeves of her dressing gown with the flourish of a conjurer, the Countess snapped, "Yes, Grimston, urgent does not begin to describe this atrocity." Fina noticed her Chelsea-bun hair had finally given way and it looked as if it were ready to attack the nearest victim.

"Dearest Alma," said the Earl – who had the adjoining bedroom, as Fina remembered – put his arm on his wife's shoulder. "Begin from the beginning, please."

With a sharp intake of breath, the Countess exhaled a stream of words. "I was just drifting off to sleep when I heard footsteps outside my door. Then the doorknob began to turn. When it did not give way – as I had locked it – the doorknob began to rattle violently. Then the door shook. Obviously someone was throwing their weight against the door to knock it down. It was horrible!"

The Earl squeezed her shoulder, encouraging her to continue.

"Fortunately, I had blocked it with a heavy desk before retiring for the night. During this time I pulled the bell pull frantically. I was so terrified that I couldn't scream."

"Calm yourself, my dear," said the Earl. Turning to Grimston, he said, "Did you see anyone in the corridor when you rushed to the Countess' door?"

"No, milord. I am afraid I did not see the malefactor," intoned Grimston. Despite the seriousness of the situation, Fina smiled inwardly at the choice of his words.

Grimston peered at the carpet and bent to retrieve an object. He straightened up to reveal a thread in his hand. He held it out for all to see. It was green. To Fina's trained eye, it looked like it was a thread from a tweed item of clothing.

Ruby took the thread from Grimston and rubbed it between her index finger and thumb rapidly. It did not pull apart. She peered at it more closely and then handed it around to the rest of the gathering to inspect.

"I think it's best we all return to our rooms," said the Earl, quietly. "We need not wake the other guests. We'll assume they have barricaded themselves in as well. That is the best we can do. Grimston and Charles, I want you two to stay up all night on guard. I suggest you keep your watch on this floor as it will be easier to travel either upstairs or downstairs. You should stay together and take turns sleeping," he said, pointing to a large decorative sofa outside the Countess' door.

"Yes, milord," said Charles and Grimston in unison.

Bleary-eyed and bedraggled, Ruby and Fina returned to Fina's room. The fire gave out a dying spark that made them both jump.

"I'm going to stay up the rest of the night, Feens," said Ruby as she began to pace in a small looping pattern in front of the fireplace.

Speaking through a yawn, Fina said, "Why would you do that? We need rest for tomorrow. Besides, I don't think I could do it." She flopped down on the bed on her back. She could feel her limbs melting into the soft eiderdown.

"Because... because... well, for two reasons. You can go to sleep – I'll stop pacing in a minute and will install myself in your chair. The first reason is that I think someone might try to attack us, or at least search our rooms. If I hear anything going on in my room, I can be there in a flash."

"And the second reason?"

"I'll tell you, but you have to promise not to protest once you know. Promise?"

"Yes! I promise."

"I still have to think on it, but I'm fairly certain I know the identity of the murderer."

34

"Ruby, wake up!" said Fina as she shook her friend lightly in the chair. So much for staying awake all night. She felt guilty – Ruby looked so peaceful in her blue silk sleeping scarf, wound around her head. She felt doubly guilty as this situation was so often reversed, Fina sleeping in and Ruby awake at the proverbial crack of dawn.

"What? Umph. What time is it?" Ruby said. "And why are you the one waking me? That's supposed to be my routine," she said with a blurry smile.

"I couldn't sleep last night. It didn't help that you wouldn't let me in on your secret," Fina said, pretend-pouting with her lower lip stuck out at an angle.

"Silly, I told you I needed to think about it..." said Ruby, mumbling. She drifted off again into unconsciousness.

Deciding this called for extreme measures, Fina marched over to the bedside to fetch her one of the two steaming cups of tea on a breakfast tray. She returned to the chair and let the smell of the tea waft under her nose. "I went down to breakfast to bring this to you especially," she said.

With an exasperated sigh, Ruby opened her eyes. "You win,

Feens. I shall awaken." She straightened up and arranged a pillow behind her back. Then, as she gracefully piloted the cup of tea to her lips, a look of pleasure spread across her face. It was as if someone had turned on an electric torch, thought Fina.

"Now, what do you want to know?" Ruby said, casually.

"What do you mean what do I want to know? Who the murderer is, of course!" said Fina playfully, though the note of impatience was not completely absent from her voice.

"Ah, yes. Well, I cannot answer that. Or at least not for certain until I have a look in the Countess' wardrobe."

Fina blinked. "The Countess' wardrobe? But the poison was in Julia's wardrobe – surely that's what you mean. You'd better drink your tea so your brain will begin to function properly."

"It's functioning perfectly, thank you," said Ruby with a mischievous smirk. "I meant what I said. Do you think you can arrange with your boyfriend – I mean Charles – for me to have a quick peek?"

"You are the limit, dear Ruby. Yes, by all means," she said with an exaggerated sigh. "Then will you tell me the identity of the murderer?" she said as if she were a small child begging for just one more iced lolly.

"Perhaps," said Ruby. Responding to Fina's hurt look on her face, she continued, "It's not that I don't want to tell you my suspicions. It's just that it's better this way. I need to gauge some reactions to see how we should proceed. And since I'm the one who would be ultimately tried for these murders if and when those ghastly police ever arrive, I think it is appropriate that I am the one who gets to decide. I am afraid that you might inadvertently reveal something to Charles before the time is right. Even if you stay silent, your face is so expressive and beautiful that you might give something away."

She laid a hand on Fina's hand.

"Well," said Fina reluctantly, "I suppose I understand. But you have to know it is terribly maddening for me."

"Yes, I understand. You will know soon, very soon," she said, draining the last bit of tea from her cup. "As will the rest of the household. But I can't say a word until we've got everyone together, in the right frame of mind to listen."

"How should I act? And how much do we tell?"

"I expect we'll have to tell a great deal. If I nod in your direction, you can assume it's safe to tell what you know, including why we're really here this weekend."

"You don't think the killer will try to harm you once you reveal their secret?"

Ruby looked thoughtful. "No," she said in a whisper, "I think I've taken precautions in that area."

A deep sigh came from Fina, half of relief, half of frustration. After looking again at her forlorn companion, Ruby said, "All right. I'll give you a clue. My suspicions were confirmed by the colour green."

At this, Fina could only stare. Her own little grey cells, she felt, were failing her miserably. She took another sip of tea in the hope that the stimulation would bring enlightenment.

A short time later, at Ruby's request, Charles and Fina stood guard in the hallway while she searched the Countess' room. Fina noticed the sun was streaming through the outside hall windows. It was a robust sunshine, not the sickly pale sunshine of late, pushing through the snow flurries. It made her feel hopeful until she realized it meant the snow would melt. The snow had been their downfall and their protection. Without it, the police would arrive.

She felt a rising anxiety, moving through her stomach up through her shoulders and her neck. She felt lightheaded. The police. The memories. Charles must have noticed her distress as he turned toward her and lightly touched her shoulder. He said,

"Are you ill, Fina? Here, come sit down." He guided her to the nearest chair. Her head felt better, but she still had a knot in her stomach and what felt like clamps on her neck and shoulders.

"I expect it's nervous anticipation," she said. "I just want this whole business to end."

Ruby slipped out of the door at that moment. Her face was set in a grim line. "It's as I expected. Let's go down to breakfast. I assume everyone is assembled there, Charles?"

He nodded and they marched slowly, as if following a funeral coffin down the stairs.

As promised, everyone was assembled in the dining room for breakfast. The same smells that had so entranced Fina that first morning at Pauncefort now made her slightly queasy. As she and Ruby settled at the table, they both only took tea and some lightly buttered toast. The atmosphere was glum, despite the sun. Conversation was sporadic and hushed.

The Earl, ever the jovial host, tried to put the party at ease. "The sun's out today and that means the police will arrive. I must say I never thought that would be good news, but dash it all if it isn't. They'll find the green man." An anaemic murmur of agreement went around the table.

Finishing her last slice of toast, Ruby put down her napkin and slid back her chair. Standing up, she proclaimed, "As we all seem to be finished with breakfast, I propose we reconvene in the saloon. I have some important news to share with you about the murders – I know who committed these crimes, and it certainly was not the elusive so-called green man. It was one of us."

Cyril and Julia gasped. Charlotte blinked. The two sisters stared at one another in wonderment. Edgar remained still, clearly still suffering the double effect of alcohol and the assault. Ian sat still with his hands folded neatly in his lap.

The Earl banged on the table. "What do you mean, you have

news about the murderer, Miss Dove? Have you been holding this back from us?" he yelled, his face turning crimson.

Ruby said in a calm voice. "I assure you, Lord Snittlegarth, I just had my suspicions confirmed this morning. Fina and I will join you all in the saloon in thirty minutes."

35

Charles had arranged the chairs and sofas in a semicircle around the fireplace. It looked like they were convening a council of war, thought Fina's political-historian brain.

Everyone, with the exception of Julia, was dressed in rather sombre navy, brown and dark grey tones. Julia looked defiant in a tangerine silk, low-cut blouse and high-waisted charcoal slacks. Fina took her place on an end chair, facing directly across from Charles and diagonally from Ruby. Ruby stood at the fireplace, hand laid on the mantel, resplendent in a cream-coloured form-fitting dress of silk crêpe. Despite the obvious toll the last few days had taken on her face, she looked ready for the coming storm – quite marvellous, thought Fina.

Everyone sat with their feet planted firmly on the floor. It looked as if they were waiting for the impact of a runaway train, she thought.

Ruby took a sip of her tea, placed it on the mantel and then pursed her lips. Her voice was quite soft at first, like a floating feather, falling to the ground. "Thank you all for agreeing to be here together. I know it appears frightfully melodramatic, but discussing murder demands this type of collective attention."

Cyril snarled, "Fancy yourself a detective as well as a fashion designer, Miss Dove?"

"Watch your tone, sir," said Ian half rising out of his seat. "Do you have any better ideas?"

Cyril shot back, "That's what I thought the police were for, my dear fellow."

Ian snorted and muttered under his breath, "Police."

Everyone began to shift in their seats.

Lady Snittlegarth put out a calming hand toward the middle of the room. They all fell quiet. Fina was impressed again by the alternating slightly-batty yet iron maiden persona of the Countess.

"Thank you, Countess," said Ruby, smoothing her dress. "I will spend time exploring what Fina, Charles and I have found with regards to these murders. I'm sure we'd all rather clear this up before the police arrive."

Putting it this way, Ruby's words had a pacifying effect on the crowd. Shoulders visibly softened, and clenched hands relaxed.

"Let us begin with the purpose of this weekend. Fina and I were invited both as guests, but also as dress designers for our clients, Lady Charlotte and Julia Aston," Ruby said, looking at the two women who nodded their agreement. "Perhaps we can briefly review the other reasons you all had for your invitation to join the weekend at Pauncefort."

Cyril sat to Fina's right, so he began his explanation. "I was invited by my student and mentee, Edgar. We know one another through Oxford. As I explained previously, he has been supporting the initiation of a professorship, funded by the Sykes-Duckworth family. I would be a beneficiary of that bequest."

Gayatri stopped moving her index finger rhythmically on her nose – lost in thought, Fina noticed. Lightly putting her arm on her sister's shoulder, she said, "As I explained to Fina the first night, I know Granville and Edgar as acquaintances at Oxford. Sajida has been staying with me on her visit to England, so I asked permission to bring her along with me. It was meant to be her first experience of a real English Yuletide festival... but..." Her voice trailed off.

Ruby interjected, "You also had met Ian before this weekend, correct?"

Gayatri gave a somewhat shy, gentle nod.

Julia leaned forward in her chair, looking straight at Ruby. "I'm not exactly sure who issued the invitation, sweetie... in my crowd, it is just something that happens. Granville, Leslie and I did cross paths – as one does – a few times. I think Ian suggested I come down this weekend."

Ian gently rubbed his hands on his thighs. "Did I, darling? I must have..." he said in a rather unconvincing manner, thought Fina.

"I think we shall return to that inconsistency later, Julia, when we discus motives for these murders," said Ruby, in a matter-of-fact tone.

Julia gave a tight smile and eased back into the sofa.

"I was invited by Granville to discuss the funding of my productions," said Ian, defiant. "I also met Leslie one or two times – probably at Ciro's Club in London."

"And as for Mr Dashwood, we know that he was a... *very...* close friend of Granville's, correct, Charlotte and Edgar?" asked Ruby.

"Yes, that's correct," said Charlotte. "Leslie often motored down for the weekend with Granville." There was no trace of irony in her voice, Fina noticed. How odd: hadn't she had suspicions about their relationship?

"Fine," said Ruby. "We obviously do not need to establish the reasons for the family to be at their own home for the weekend. Let us proceed to a recounting of the crimes."

"Must we go through this all again, Miss Dove?" asked Edgar. He rubbed the back of his head where he had been hit.

Ignoring the interruption, Ruby continued. "On Friday evening, sometime after I announced the existence of a deadly poison in my possession – or I should say in my room – someone purloined that poison from my room. Though we initially thought Granville's brandy snifter or his hot cocoa must have been laced with the poison, we now know that was not the case. The murderer crept up to my room, pilfered the poison and then inserted the poison in Granville's tooth powder container. We can assume the poisoner did not know a great deal about the effects of oxalic acid. That is why they emptied most of the tooth powder to ensure the full and immediate effect of the poison."

Taken aback, Fina had to work to keep her surprise from showing on her face. They had never found the tooth powder container. How did Ruby know? Was she bluffing?

Charlotte interjected, "But Granville was fastidious about everything – particularly his personal hygiene. Wouldn't he have noticed that the tooth powder container was nearly empty?"

Gayatri answered, "Yes, but remember he was quite inebriated. He probably wouldn't have noticed."

"I agree," said Ruby. "With the little re-enactment we had last night, we established that nearly everyone had the opportunity to slip up to my room and Granville's bathroom to set the stage for the murder. Granville was the last one to retire for the night. He must have brushed his teeth and then retired to bed – where he died."

"Just a moment, m'dear," said the Earl. Ruby flashed a look of annoyance at the term. Fina noticed that he was oblivious or indifferent to her facial response. "How do you know that he was the last one to retire for the night? What were you doing up and about?" He looked triumphant, as if he had just cornered his quarry and was now ready to pounce.

Not missing a beat, Ruby responded, "Fina and I were in the library looking for books to read. We were both unable to sleep."

Fina nodded as proof to support her friend's assertion, but noticed by the expressions on the faces of the assembled guests that they were unconvinced by this explanation.

"Next, we come to the murder of Leslie Dashwood. Unlike Granville, Mr Dashwood was found face down on the floor of his bedroom, facing away from the entrance to his bathroom. We discovered two items of interest in that crime. First was the discovery of the method of delivering the poison in both murders – the tooth powder. Leslie had obviously just come from the bathroom before he died, so we checked to see if there were traces of oxalic acid on the toothbrush. There were. Accordingly, Fina went to Granville's bathroom to see if she could find the same evidence for his murder. As we all know, she was assaulted when she tried to do this. I think it is safe to assume that she was getting too close to the truth for our murderer."

Fina said, "I also heard a conversation between Julia and Sajida before I was coshed on the head. Though I'm a little fuzzy about the conversation, I do remember hearing Julia say, 'I can't believe he's gone...' then Sajida's voice said in a hush, 'Yes, he won't bother us any more'."

A collective gasp went around the room. All eyes turned to Julia and Sajida. Both looked defiant. Sajida said, "I cannot see what this private conversation has to do with the murder."

Fina replied, feeling the anger rise up from her stomach, "Well, it does seem to suggest you had a good reason for wishing Leslie out of the way. Besides, how do we know you didn't hit me on the head when you realized I'd heard your conversation?"

Sajida's defiant look melted away. Julia responded by taking up the task of response. In marked contrast to her usual bombast, Julia nearly whispered, "You see, Leslie Dashwood was simply a horrid man. Sajida and I met at a party and became fast friends. We bonded, initially, over our stories of Leslie's... behaviour." Julia faltered.

Fina gave an involuntary shudder. She could feel what was coming.

Sajida continued, the spoiled princess act – if it were an act – now vanished. "Leslie Dashwood was a fiend. A fiend of the worst type. One who preys on women. Assault. That is the best word for it in polite company. Julia and I did come to Pauncefort with the intention to take our revenge."

Gayatri's mouth opened as wide as one of the Countess' ornamental fish. Looking at her sister, Sajida continued, "Yes, my sister did not know what had happened to us – or about our thirst for revenge. But you must believe us that we came only with our anger and injury. We did not have a plan, and certainly did not commit either of the murders. The conversation you heard, Fina, was about how our problem – if you will – had been solved. We never would hurt anyone – not physically, at least."

36

It was so silent they all could hear the faint wheeze of the Earl's breath. Then Fina sensed a shift of energy in the room. There was an air of prurient – no, salacious – interest that hung in the ether.

Ruby said, "That seems plausible, and from what we know of Leslie's behaviour, it certainly seems in keeping with his character. I must say I had no idea it went that far, however. Let us leave this aside for a moment and continue on with the recounting of events. We know that anyone in the house could have committed the second murder. During the course of the day, anyone could have entered Leslie's bathroom and inserted the poison in the tooth powder or the toothbrush. Remember, we did not know at this point that the method of delivering the poison was through the tooth powder, so Leslie would have had no reason to be wary of brushing his teeth."

Then Ruby pulled the locket and broken chain out of her blue clutch on the mantel. "We have one other item relevant to the murders," she said, holding it aloft so everyone could see.

Charles chimed in. "Miss Badarur and I found that locket

with the broken chain on Leslie's body after the murder was committed."

"The locket is empty, but it is engraved, as you can see," Ruby said, pointing to the centre of the locket, "with a large letter C." She then passed the necklace to Charles who proceeded to hand it around the group.

"Shouldn't we have left it alone for fingerprinting by the police?" asked the Earl.

"Yes, we thought of that, but when Charles removed the locket from the pocket of Leslie's dinner jacket, he had already placed his hand around it, thus removing the possibility of useful fingerprints... Beyond that," said Ruby in a low voice, "I hope we won't need to rely on the police for a confession." She hurried on before anyone could object to her statement. "As this appears to be a woman's necklace, we assumed that the C must refer to the initials of a woman. Though having a name that begins with the letter C is hardly damning evidence, it is suggestive."

"So, out with it, Ruby," said Cyril impatiently.

Ignoring him, she continued. "Besides the obvious Lady Charlotte, the Countess' middle name is Christine and Julia's is Cicely."

"So what?" said Julia. "It doesn't prove a bloody thing, sweetie."

Ruby nodded. "As I said, it is merely suggestive. It is peculiar that Leslie would have this in his dinner jacket pocket. It may be completely unrelated, nevertheless it is an important clue to consider." She cleared her throat and continued. "So far, we have two murders and one physical assault on my dear friend, Fina. Next, we come to the re-enactment. Edgar suffered a concussion to the head—"

"I did not suffer a concussion, Miss Dove. Someone hit me

on the head with murderous intent," said Edgar in a burst of anger.

"Quite right. This assault was rather convenient – and I use that word in a purposeful manner – in that it allowed us to narrow down the list of suspects. When I thought back to the wide-open field of opportunity for committing these crimes, I thought this attack on you to be most intriguing. The other crimes were committed so that suspicion was cast on everyone. I thought this was quite ingenious from the murderer's perspective. We often read about so-and-so having been framed for a crime. That seems to be often the case – the murderer tries to frame a particular individual for a crime."

"But that is a risky strategy," said Fina.

"Exactly, Fina," said Ruby. "It is much easier to hide in a crowd than point the finger at someone, because so often it is easier to trace who is instigating the finger pointing. No, it is ingenious precisely because everyone is suspected, and therefore no one can be responsible! That is why this attack on Edgar struck me as odd. It seemed a deliberate attempt to narrow the field of suspects to just a few people: Cyril, Charlotte and Julia."

Ian interjected, "Are you saying that the attack on Edgar was unrelated? Or not committed by the murderer? Does that mean we have *two* mad people plus this apparent mystery green man?"

"Ah yes, the madman. I will come to that in a moment. As for the attack on Edgar, I do believe it is connected to the murder, but was not committed by the murderer themselves."

"Do you mean an accomplice?" spluttered the Earl.

"Perhaps. But I'm thinking more along the line of someone who wants to protect the murderer," replied Ruby.

The Earl stared at her, dumbfounded. "I confess I am becoming more confused than enlightened, Miss Dove."

Ruby smiled. "I know. I want to lay out all the possibilities so we can arrive at a crystal clear conclusion. Now, let's assume for the moment that the attack on Edgar was committed to narrow the list of suspects. We have yet another diversionary attempt with the citing of this supposed madman on the loose in Pauncefort Hall."

Lady Charlotte and the Countess began to speak at once. Charlotte let her aunt proceed. "But Charlotte saw the madman, and I have evidence that he tried to get into my room!" the Countess shrieked.

"I understand, Lady Snittlegarth, but that was a ruse as well," Ruby said in a calm and steady voice. "Both the attack on Edgar and the sighting of the rather convenient madman were diversions from the murders. However, let's return to these events later – otherwise we'll be distracted from the truth of this affair itself. Let's review the reasons why the murders might have been committed. Fina, would you be so good as to help me with this portion? I should say at the outset that we'll come to our own reasons at the end. Don't worry, I shall leave out nothing." She motioned to Fina.

Fina cleared her throat and pulled out her notebook. Reading aloud in a rather wooden tone to begin, she soon found her rhythm. "Cyril Lighton. Professor at Oxford. Friend and mentor to Edgar. Leftist political beliefs. In line to be the recipient of prestigious new professorship endowed by Granville. Granville, an active Fascist, threatened to withdraw funds for the professorship once he found out someone holding leftist political beliefs would be the recipient of the professorship. Political beliefs alone could have been the motive, but I think we all agree that is a little weak. But certainly people have killed for less than a prestigious named professorship at Oxford. Cyril is one of the few people who could conceivably have committed all of the crimes – including the somewhat dubious assault against Edgar—"

Cyril's face screwed up in a little red clutch of skin. "We've been through all this before. Nothing new here."

"Yes, that's true, Professor Lighton, but that doesn't change the facts," said Ruby. She turned her head away from Cyril to indicate the transition to the next suspect.

Fina continued. "Ian Clavering. Successful producer. Invited by Granville to discuss prospects of funding productions. Ian knew Granville was set to come into a great deal of money, so he was priming him for this venture. Ian also has a relationship with Julia, so he may have sought revenge on her behalf."

Ian said coolly, "Though chivalry isn't dead, I would never commit that type of murder. My motive would have to be much stronger."

"Yes, indeed, Ian," said Ruby, almost faltering.

Fina continued. "Next we have Gayatri Badarur. Student of medicine at Oxford. Her younger sister, Sajida, is visiting from India. Both sisters had the chance to commit the crime, assuming the assault on Edgar was a separate incident. Sajida wished to take revenge on Leslie Dashwood – we do not know if Gayatri knew or did not know about Leslie's crimes – we only have her verbal assurances of this. If they were in it together, perhaps even with Julia, then this could become a three-person crime.

"In any case, there's also the matter of Lavington's plantation holdings in Assam. We discovered this connection after finding a report in Edgar's room that related to Dulcet & Sons. They have plantations in Assam, an area presided over by the Badarurs, which Lavington's have their eye on. It would be an evil day for Nowgong if the purchase of those plantations went through, and I believe Edgar – and the Badarur sisters – were well aware of that."

"Good God – have you been searching our rooms?" the Earl interjected.

"All will be explained in due course, Lord Snittlegarth. Please let's continue on this thread at the moment."

Looking somewhat mollified, the Earl sat back and waved his hand to continue.

"Thank you, Fina and Ruby. I will explain it myself, if you don't mind," said Gayatri, sitting fully erect with her hands placed delicately in her lap. Fina nodded her assent.

Gayatri proceeded to recount the same story she had shared with Ruby and Fina earlier in the library.

In wrapping up her explanation, she said, "However, as I explained to Fina and Ruby when they questioned us earlier about this, we did not come here this weekend seeking revenge – at least not for this reason," Gayatri said, looking pointedly at her sister. "Moreover, neither my sister nor I have the physical urge to violence. If we did actually feel that inclination, I assure you we have enough connections that we could hire someone to carry out an assassination, if necessary."

Fina happened to glance over at Charles, whose face indicated he found this assertion plausible. Scanning the rest of the room, Fina could see that most of the company appeared to be placated by this explanation.

Fina could tell from Ruby's body language that it was time for her to continue. "Moving forward, we come to Julia Aston. Actress and socialite. Friend of Ian Clavering. Also Ruby's client this weekend. Had the opportunity to commit both murders, as well as the assaults on Fina and Edgar. We explored Julia's feelings regarding Leslie Dashwood earlier."

Julia sniffed, in a highly theatrical manner. "Leslie was a rotter, I'll give you that. But that doesn't make me a murderer, darling."

"What about the poison Charles found in the back of your wardrobe, Julia?" asked Fina, hoping to catch her off guard.

Julia glared at Charles. He shrugged his shoulders in return.

"I, I, didn't do it," stammered the normally silver-tongued Julia.

"Well?" said Cyril.

Ruby held up her hand as if in explanation. "I believe Julia hid the poison to protect someone. It was Ian, wasn't it?"

Julia nodded miserably. Ian's eyes goggled. He looked at her as if he had seen her for the first time.

With her head buried in her hands, she said, "I thought Ian had done it, so I hid the poison in the back of my wardrobe. You see, I heard about the locket – and knew that Ian kept his mother's locket with him – her name was Cynthia."

"That's true, but I still have my mother's locket... but how did you come into possession of the poison?" asked Ian.

"I found it on your nightstand when I went in to search for the locket. I panicked and hid it in my wardrobe," she replied.

Ian gulped. "I swear, I swear..."

"I know you didn't do it, Ian," said Ruby, gently.

"But you just heard that Julia found the poison in his room!" screeched Cyril.

"Yes, but someone else put it there to incriminate him," she replied.

Scanning the room, Fina saw that no one moved. Not even a facial muscle.

Ruby continued. "Before we move on to members of the family, let us discuss the members of the staff. Though any member of the staff had the chance to commit these crimes, everyone has been in service at Pauncefort for many years. The question we have to ask ourselves, then, is, why now? There seems to be no easy answer to this. There has not been any major family revelation – at least not publicly to the staff – and the family is here quite often so opportunities would abound. Moreover, the dreadful weather has made this the worst possible weekend to commit a murder: there's only a small pool of suspects. Much better to wait when the crimes could be blamed on an outside interloper."

Ruby paused. "The one exception to this is Charles Frett."

Fina noticed Grimston's lips purse, almost imperceptibly.

"When Charles drove us to Pauncefort from the station, Fina and I both noticed that he had a particular reaction to the fact we were both at Oxford. Charles' manner and speech patterns seemed to indicate that he might have been at a place such as Oxford at one time – or at least prepared to go to Oxford. This, coupled with the fact that he has been employed at Pauncefort for just ten months, made us suspicious. When we pressed him about his life story, we found out that he had indeed been on the verge of going to Oxford. His chance had been taken away from him, however, by a prison sentence given by none other than Justice Henry Sykes-Duckworth, father of Charlotte, Edgar and Granville," said Ruby.

By this time, Charles' face was quite red. He said nothing.

"Charles did divulge that he took the job with the intention of seeking revenge on Henry Sykes-Duckworth. However, he found that he liked the work here and that his will to actually do anything – at least in a physical sense – had been sapped," said Ruby.

"It's true," said Charles. "I actually found that although I was still bitter about losing my place at Oxford, the work here suited me quite well. Besides this, killing Granville would have only lost me a job since he had threatened to sell Pauncefort once he had his inheritance."

The Earl and his wife traded uneasy glances. Charlotte, too, seemed to become even more guarded in her manner. Only the guests – Cyril, Julia, Ian and the Badarurs – showed any sign of surprise.

"And it is that last point – about inheritances – that brings us to discussing the motives of the family," said Ruby.

37

"Let us begin with the Earl and Countess of Snittlegarth. Lady and Lord Snittlegarth have, for all intents and purposes, raised their nieces and nephews. After Lady Sykes-Duckworth died, these responsibilities fell on the shoulders of the two of them, mostly because Justice Sykes-Duckworth's legal career continued its upward trajectory," said Ruby, looking at Lord and Lady Snittlegarth.

The Earl responded, nodding his head. "Yes, after dear Catherine's untimely death, Alma and I became the de facto parents of the household. In addition to his legal career, as you say, Miss Dove, Henry had to attend to the business in the Caribbean as well. It was more than a full-time job. Henry – as difficult as he can be – did recognize the immense burden this placed on us, and gave us free rein at Pauncefort Hall."

"As a result, you feel particularly protective of your nieces and nephews. You also must have been alarmed by Granville's declaration that he would sell Pauncefort once he inherited the estate," said Ruby.

Charlotte came to their defence. "That is true, but Auntie and Uncle would never harm Granville. He was like a son – as you said. No matter how difficult he might be, family is family."

Ruby turned suddenly on Charlotte. "This applies to you as well, Lady Charlotte. You also would be turned out of your home without a penny upon your father's death. Granville might have given you an annual allowance, but given his personality we can assume it would be a grudging one at best. You would struggle to make an advantageous marriage, and without funds, you could hardly live in the style to which you've become accustomed. It is enough to make even the most loving sister desperate. You, too, might have wanted Granville out of the way."

Though she remained perfectly composed, Fina saw Charlotte's eyes flash with an anger she hadn't seen before. "You may very well think that, but you haven't any proof."

"Be that as it may," said Ruby, turning away from Charlotte. "But you are still among the top suspects. I'm sure the police wouldn't have much trouble building a case against you."

"Leave off my sister!" shouted Edgar, his voice echoing his puffed out chest for the first time. "She cannot be a murderer. I know her too well. She's tough as nails, but would never hurt a fly."

"And now we come to the last suspect. Edgar. Little brother to Granville and Charlotte. Always protected from the worst of the family – particularly its secrets. Because we know that every family has its secrets. And the secrets of the Snittlegarths and the Sykes-Duckworths are particularly horrible. But no more or less horrible than any other aristocratic colonial-imperial family in England," said Ruby, her voice gaining in volume.

The Earl, who looked as if he were going to keel over for at least the fifth time during these proceedings, turned a particularly striking shade of vermillion upon hearing this. "Miss Dove, did I hear you correctly? This family hasn't any secrets – at least none worth a scandal of any kind. And as for that claptrap about colonial-imperial family, I have to assume at this point that it is Bolshie nonsense of some kind. Are you a spy for the reds?!"

Fina and Ruby exchanged glances. Fina wondered if she should step in to explain, but could tell from the iron look on Ruby's face that she should await further instructions before diving into this morass.

Smoothing her skirt and wetting her lips, Ruby continued. "Your statement is correct in one sense of the word, Lord Snittlegarth. Fina and I are engaged in intelligence gathering of a sort. It is this intelligence gathering that led us here this weekend, and ultimately provided the necessary evidence needed to sort out these crimes."

Clearing her throat to cover her nervousness, Ruby continued. "The Earls of Snittlegarth and Malvern – that is, the Sykes-Duckworth families – have owned plantations in the Caribbean and in India, among other areas of the world. We already discussed their interests in India. In the Caribbean, they are owners of a planation on my family's home island of St Kitts."

She extracted an envelope from her clutch and held it up. "These papers, hidden in the study, describe certain atrocities committed at Bluegate in St Kitts a year ago – with full backing from this family. Or, should I say, Lavington's to be more precise. My cousin was one of the victims."

As Ruby looked rather exhausted by this point, Fina cleared her throat and continued on. "Ruby and I were tasked with coming here this weekend to find these incriminating papers describing this series of horrific crimes on the plantation. Our aim was to then turn over these papers to a group of people in London and St Kitts – of which we are a part – fighting against the conditions of the plantations."

"People?" echoed the Earl, as though repeating the word would make it more comprehensible. "People? What people?"

"People fighting against British colonialism, Lord Snittle-garth. Fina and I are part of group – or I should say web of inter-connected people – though we know little about everyone involved. That is to protect us all in case the British government gets wind of it."

Looking around, Fina saw that the Earl and Countess were startled to the point of bafflement as to why anyone would want to fight against British colonialism. Ian and Julia, however, were exchanging a knowing glance, and Cyril was nodding smugly. Her spirits rose. So they had some allies, after all.

She went on: "Though we had little hope of prompting any official enquiry into these crimes, the hope was to create such a scandal that the Sykes-Duckworths would have to close the plantation. We did this at the request of those living on the plantation themselves. Conditions are such that although closure would mean the loss of livelihood for some, it is far better to close. There are hopes of eventually reclaiming the land."

Nodding, Ruby picked up the next thread. "So you see, we were in the study searching for these papers on the first night – the night that Granville was poisoned. That is how we knew about the argument between Cyril, Granville and Edgar. In fact," she added, "we must have been very nearly the last ones to see Granville alive."

Scanning the room, Fina saw that the universal body language was one of slack jaws and protruding eyeballs.

"Of course, some of you may be wondering if this gave me a reason to kill Granville myself," said Ruby coolly. "I need hardly state that it was unnecessary to do so because I found the papers in question, which would ultimately prove more satisfying than any need to resort to physical violence."

Cyril barked out, "But what if Granville discovered the real reason you and Miss Aubrey-Havelock were down here this weekend? That would give you reason to shut him up, as our American friends would say."

"Even if that were true – which it wasn't, at least to my knowledge – I certainly wouldn't implicate myself with the use of my own poison. Besides, we all know that given the way prejudice works in this country, I certainly would be at the top of the police list of suspects. Moreover, even if Granville had found out, what could he have done? Expose me? That would only lead to the scandal which he wished to avoid."

Julia jumped in. "But what about Fina? She could have done it on your behalf."

Ruby began to speak, but Fina was ready to defend herself. "I could have, but again, I would be implicating my best friend, and partner in this business. Besides that, we all know I couldn't cosh myself on my own head." Anticipating another objection, Fina continued, "And if we were in it together – for the sake of argument – we'd hardly implicate ourselves with the use of Ruby's poison."

The Countess leapt to her feet with a broad grin on her face. "Aha!" she declared. "But what if the aim was to murder Leslie, rather than the other way around? Murder him for his political beliefs – which are obviously quite different than your own."

"That is a clever possibility, Countess, but one that is rather far-fetched. Even though Fina and I – as well as a few others in this room – found Mr Dashwood's political activities odious, he would have also been potentially exposed by his associations with Granville. Such as they were," said Ruby.

Silence.

Fina's stomach muscles tensed, and she decided she had better speak. "I do have one more motive, one that is unconnected to St Kitts. You see, my brother was Connor Aubrey-Havelock."

She scanned the room for a reaction. All faces looked blank, except one.

"Of course! I knew there was a reason something about you seemed vaguely familiar." The voice came from Ian Clavering. "Your brother was hanged for the murder of your father, correct?" His look of satisfaction turned quickly to one of shame as he realized the import of his statement.

"Yes, that's correct. Some of you may now remember the case. It was three years ago," said Fina, fighting back the rising tide of emotion. "The relevant points here are that, first, I know my brother did not murder my father. I could tell you all the lurid details of police and legal misconduct, but you can read about them yourself in the sensational newspaper accounts. The point is that not only was my brother not guilty, but there were several grave miscarriages of so-called justice before and after the trial."

"I remember now," said Cyril quietly. "The judge was Henry Sykes-Duckworth, was it not?"

Fina nodded, unable to utter the words 'yes'. She sat back in her chair with a thud.

Ruby sat down on the edge of the chair and whispered into Fina's ear, "Do you want me to continue?" Fina nodded and gave a weak smile.

Ruby held her hand on Fina's shoulder as she moved to stand. "Justice Sykes-Duckworth's pronouncement in the case was particularly vulgar and spiteful. He seemed to take positive glee in the pronouncement of a death sentence. Nevertheless, Fina did not murder Granville. Like Charles, she would have had a different target: Lord Malvern, that is, Henry Sykes-Duckworth himself. Fina did not know what the relationship was like between the judge and his offspring, so she could hardly have known one way or another whether losing a son would have hurt him as much as the loss of her brother hurt her family."

Now standing tall, Ruby made a noticeable shift in her speech. "This story, along with my own, provides the context of my proposal. You see, Fina and I became friends over the ways in which the so-called justice system of this colonial-imperial power operates. In the case of Fina, it was one of overstepping and in mine it was quite the opposite. What our cases shared, however, was prejudice and violence. Fina's mother was Irish and practically disowned from the aristocratic family into which she married. The police and news reporters played on anti-Irish sentiment – implying and sometimes just stating explicitly that Fina's brother was naturally violent because he was Irish. Lord Malvern played into this as well in his statements from the bench. This Bluegate affair, of mass murder on the part of a white Britisher going not only unprosecuted but simply unnoticed and ignored, is a parallel process, though one that had different results."

Now it was Charlotte who interrupted. Fina saw her eyes widen. It was a look of pure terror. "What, Ruby, does this all have to do with the murder of my brother and Leslie? I must confess that I knew nothing of our family's involvement in what you described."

"I know you did not know about this violence, but you must have known about the violence in your family. Why else would you shield a murderer?" asked Ruby.

"I, I, I don't know what you are referring to, I'm sure," said Charlotte. Stammering, she balled up her graceful hands in her lap to keep them from shaking.

"Ruby, I do hope you will leave off my sister," said Edgar in a low voice. "I'm warning you."

Ruby spun around to face Edgar directly. "I suppose I would do well to take heed of a warning from a murderer."

In contrast to other moments of stunning revelation, everyone began chattering at once. The Countess stood up, and with a dramatic flap of her arms as if she were about to take flight, she silenced everyone. "Miss Dove, I do wish you would stop all of this nonsensical blather. The police should be here quite soon, I'm sure."

"Yes, that is why it is of the utmost urgency that everyone stay calm and quiet. I do want to continue with my proposal. First, let me detail the actual crimes committed by Edgar. Then I will proceed to a proposal that I believe is in the family's best interest.

"It is best if we start the story approximately fifteen years ago, when Edgar was a boy. You see, Lady Malvern, Catherine was a warm and thoughtful mother. She was also a mother that had strong views on what was best for her children. As we all know, she died quite suddenly when Edgar was four years old. Charlotte was five and Granville was eleven. Fina and I first learned of this story through two avenues. The first was through the cook, Mrs Lynn, who told us of the family tragedy – that Lady Malvern had died of ptomaine poisoning. We heard from her that it happened soon after Granville was to be sent to boarding school. We also learned that Edgar and his mother were unusually close. That was evident from the stories of the cook and Edgar himself, as well as a photo Fina saw in Edgar's bedroom when we first arrived." Ruby opened her clutch on the mantelpiece and withdrew the happy photo of Edgar and his mother. She passed it around for all to see.

"Fina and I had already suspected Edgar of having a motive for killing his brother over the issue of the professorship. But it still seemed hardly enough to justify actually murdering one's sibling, even if relations had been strained between them over the years. There was an added edge to their argument we overheard that first night in the study. Though we did not know it at the time, the phrase 'I know what you did' was significant when Edgar uttered it accusingly at Granville. Fina and I both thought it was about the professorship or about what happened in Bluegate. When Leslie was found dead with the locket with the letter C engraved on it, a story began to form in my mind."

"You see, there was something odd about the story of Lady Sykes-Duckworth's death. The suddenness of it – the inexplicable nature of it. What if someone had murdered her, all those years ago? Her husband? Possibly, though it seemed hardly to fit the nature of the current crime. What about the two other adults in the household? Lady or Lord Snittlegarth? Again, it seemed hardly relevant to the current crime. What if Edgar's reference to 'I know what you did' was an accusation of Granville himself? After all, as the oldest child at age eleven, it seemed quite plausible. Especially as we knew that there was a major event to take place around the time of her death – Granville being sent to boarding school. Lord and Lady Snittlegarth – do you remember him being upset by this change?"

The Earl and Countess exchanged furtive glances. The Earl spoke quietly. "Yes, he was unreasonably upset by it. Of course it's normal not to want to leave, but he took it too far. Was unfortunately a mark of his character in general."

"Yes, it was an early mark of his character most certainly. Am I right in my supposition that Granville killed his mother in a fit of rage?" asked Ruby.

Again, the Earl spoke quietly. "Yes... yes, he did. Put rat poison in her tea. At the time, we all said it was due to some cherries she ate. But that wasn't the truth. Granville told us he was so cross with her that he just wanted to make her ill – not kill her. Henry, myself and Alma all knew what had happened. Henry was aggrieved and so disgusted with his children that he completely withdrew by throwing himself into his work. I'm not sure why, but Alma and I felt responsible. Not so much for Granville, but for Charlotte and Edgar. They were the unfortunate victims of this entire affair. Neither of them knew what had happened."

"You fool!" screeched the Countess, hitting her husband, sobbing. "She was merely guessing! Why did you tell her?"

Charlotte gently clutched her aunt and lifted her back into her spot on the couch. The Earl looked sheepish, but also relieved, thought Fina.

"I'm so sorry, m'dear, but it would have come out anyway. Now that Granville is dead, I had to unburden myself. I could not bear the strain any longer," said the Earl, shaking his head.

"Yes, it was wise, Lord Snittlegarth. The locket, the attack on Edgar and finally the sighting of this supposed madman on the loose in Pauncefort Hall by Lady Snittlegarth and Lady Charlotte all pointed in the direction of Edgar as the killer. By process of elimination, we knew that it was likely that the locket was attached to Lady Charlotte, Lady Snittlegarth, or Julia. When we found out the name of Granville's mother was Catherine, especially given the antique style of the piece, it seemed possible that it might have been her own locket. Is that correct, Lady Snittlegarth?"

The Countess pursed her lips and nodded.

"That means that this locket was somehow a signal about Lady Sykes-Duckworth's death. My guess is that Edgar found out – very recently – that his brother had murdered their mother. Perhaps you can enlighten us, Lady Charlotte."

She looked like a broken woman, thought Fina. Her shoulders slumped, and she was hunched over, almost doubled over.

"The last time Father came home, I overheard a conversation between him and Auntie Alma – I mean, Lady Snittlegarth," said Charlotte. "They were discussing the terms of his will. When I say it was a conversation, I should say it was an argument. Their voices were raised, which is why I heard it – I am not usually in the habit of listening at doors. My father wanted to make Granville the sole heir, and he also wanted to make him head of the company. My auntie was vehemently opposed; in fact, she was quite shocked by the suggestion. She blurted out something to the effect of 'Why would you leave everything to a murderer?'. From the rest of the conversation I could make out that what they were discussing was the murder of my mother. I was completely on the side of my auntie, obviously, and could not understand why in heaven's name Father would leave everything to Granville – especially because he had so obviously despised him when we were growing up. My father said that Granville had showed promise of late in terms of politics and management – little did he know that the family had been covering for him in various ways, as always. He thought it would make something out of him, that he had turned a corner. I suppose my father might also have felt guilty about turning his back on Granville when all this had happened. Whatever the reason, that is how I found out about what happened to my mother."

Curiously gaining strength from her tale, Charlotte straightened up a bit. "I was wild with rage. I didn't know how to confront Granville about it. I began wearing my mother's locket every day, in a visible way. I wanted to see how he would react. The first time he saw me in it he looked frightened. Then, with each passing day that I wore it around my neck, he grew increasingly enraged. Finally, he confronted me about it. He asked me why I was suddenly wearing it each day so openly. I was so angry at that moment that I said, 'You of all people should know why'. Then he tore the necklace from my neck – that's why the chain was broken. After Granville had stomped away with the necklace, Edgar came upon me to find me crying uncontrollably. My hair was dishevelled – quite out of character for me."

Edgar said quietly, "Yes, it looked like you had been in quite a dust-up, old girl."

Charlotte smiled wanly. "You see, the family had always been overprotective of Edgar and myself. It all made sense now. I felt I had to tell him. I couldn't hold it in any longer, especially because I knew how close our mother had been to Edgar as the baby of the family."

Fina asked, "When did you tell him?"

"She told me last weekend," said Edgar. "I suppose in my mind – subconsciously at least – I knew I was going to harm him. I had to have r–r–revenge. It wasn't just the murder of my mother, you see, though that certainly would have been enough. Granville had always treated me badly. The fact that the family was protective of me only seemed to encourage him to mock me. This was the last straw. When you mentioned the poison that night, Ruby, it prompted me to act. You're not responsible, though. I–I–I just thought that I would see what happened. I didn't know how fast the poison would act, or even if he would die. I knew that he would feel pain, one way or another. When he died, I h–h–hoped that everyone would take it as an accident – or perhaps even suicide, though I hadn't thought that far ahead to plan anything."

"How did you do it?" asked Julia.

Edgar had nearly folded in on himself – shrinking with shame, thought Fina. "I dashed up to Ruby's room after dinner and put the poison in my pocket. At that point, I wasn't sure if I could go through with it – but it seemed like some sort of sign that you had announced you had a poisonous substance with you, Miss Dove."

Ruby remained motionless.

"Then after I confronted my brother in the study, I went up to his bathroom and slipped the poison into his tooth powder tin and on his toothbrush. When Miss Dove and Miss Aubrey-Havelock saw me leaving the study that night, I appeared quite drunk. Though I'd had quite a bit to drink, I exaggerated how drunk I had been, just in case I happened across someone as I was executing my plan."

Some loose end was bothering Fina. Then she remembered. "There are two things I don't understand. One is a thud Ruby and I heard after Granville had gone upstairs and the other was the damp rug in the study."

"What thud?" asked Ian. "I didn't hear anything." Nods of agreement went around the circle.

"It's possible none of you heard it because Fina and I were on the ground floor," explained Ruby.

"Yes, I think I can explain, Miss Aubrey-Havelock. You see, after I had put the poison in the bathroom – and after Granville went to bed, I went a little mad. I immediately regretted what I had done, but I had no way of knowing if he had actually died. I came back downstairs to get a drink to steady my nerves. I returned to the study. I just paced back and forth in front of the fire, picturing what was happening to Granville. I panicked. For another mad moment, I thought I could just escape – Pauncefort and the murder. I opened the French doors – yes, I was unhinged at this point – and a small avalanche of snow cascaded into the study. That must have been the sound you heard. I was able to clear it enough away from the doors to close them, but was left with a large snow pile on the rug near the doors."

Cyril asked, "Why did you kill Leslie?"

Edgar just stared at his hands.

"I will hazard a guess," said Ruby. "Fina and I both sensed that Granville and Leslie were lovers. The inordinate grief-stricken response of Leslie after Granville's death seemed to confirm that supposition. I think Granville had confided in Leslie about killing his mother and the most recent fallout from the crime. He knew Edgar had begun to ferret out the truth. Leslie must have confronted Edgar about it. Edgar panicked and killed him – killed him the same way that he had killed his brother. It was risky, but he probably felt he had no other option."

Edgar nodded his head, now looking up at Ruby. "Yes... Leslie burst in on me that morning in my bedroom. H–h–he had found the locket in Granville's room and said it was proof of my crime. He said that he was going to keep it and then turn me in once the police arrived. I panicked. I know nothing about how to murder people, so I just used the same method that had worked before. I am s–s–sorry about hitting you on the head, Fina, but I did have to keep a close eye on the bathroom to make sure no one found out. I watched you take the toothbrush, and I knew I couldn't let you hand it over to the police, so I had to... to..." He bowed his head miserably.

Fina gulped, but did not move her eyes from Edgar.

"And you must have been the one to hide the poison – in plain sight – in my room," said Ian.

Edgar nodded.

The Countess interjected. "Dear Edgar is distressed, Miss Dove, and doesn't know what he is saying. You've got the poor child all in a state of terrible confusion. How could he have committed these crimes and then hit himself on the head? And what about the madman that Charlotte saw and the one who tried to enter my room last night to kill me?"

Ruby smiled. "Your attempt at protecting your family is admirable, Countess, but futile. At some point during the last few days, you and Lady Charlotte must have realized what had happened. You were afraid for Edgar and wanted to protect him – as you always have. Thus you concocted this cock-and-bull story and orchestrated the attack on Edgar."

She turned to Charlotte. "You hit Edgar on the head – though he did not know it – for his own protection. Edgar could not have possibly hit himself on the head, so you knew suspicion would be diverted elsewhere. You also fabricated that story about seeing the madman in the corridor after your aunt so helpfully introduced it into our heads. You also searched for the Bluegate papers in the study, knowing that it created motives for the murder that focused on the family."

Ruby then turned to the Countess. "As for the Countess' intruder, that was simply a clever trick by the Countess herself. I suspected as much and had my suspicions confirmed when I matched the green thread with the suit of the same textile I recognized in her wardrobe."

Charlotte let out a long, deep sigh. It was a sigh of relief, thought Fina. "Yes, you are correct, Ruby. Though my auntie and I dared not discuss it, we both sensed the same point – that Edgar had killed Granville. We played off one another quite nicely, I thought. Suspicion was diverted."

"Yes, it was a valiant effort. I think the madman story was a bit much, though. I can understand why you felt it necessary, however, as neither of you wanted to implicate any of the guests when the police arrived," said Ruby.

The Earl had his face buried in his hands. He looked up and said, "What do we do now? You said you had some sort of proposal?"

Edgar, who now resembled marble in colour and posture alike, rejoined, "Need it – need it involve..." He stopped short.

"Yes, I know. I think we all want to avoid a death sentence, Edgar. I shall explain. Fina and I first met and bonded over the trial and subsequent execution of her brother. We are both committed anti-prison and anti-death sentence advocates. We do not believe this solves any problems – it only creates more violence. That is why we are here this weekend, ultimately. We do not want any more deaths in St Kitts because of Lavington's plantation. We know that Edgar will suffer quite enough in his conscience." She looked benevolently down at Edgar's trembling frame.

"As for the family, we propose that once Lord Malvern passes away, you all immediately divest of all of your holdings overseas. I do not mean you should sell them to another rapacious business person, but rather that you should either close them entirely, or more preferably, turn it over to local control on the island. You shall make no profit from this scheme."

"Thank God. I didn't want to run that bloody company anyway," mumbled Edgar.

Ruby continued on as if Edgar hadn't spoken. "You will also turn over all relevant papers regarding the massacre in St Kitts, and any similar documentation about Nowgong, to the Badarur sisters. You will tell no one, quite obviously, your reasons for doing so. In exchange, no one here, including myself, shall ever divulge what we know of Edgar, Charlotte and the Countess' part in these crimes. It is in the best interest of all here that you do so."

Cyril – ever the irritating guest, thought Fina – spoke up. "But why should we – the other guests – keep quiet?"

Ruby's eyes flashed in anger. "Because if you do not, you may easily find yourself in the dock, Professor Lighton. That goes for everyone here. If anyone dares to violate this agreement, you may find yourself at the centre of a police enquiry. Fina and I know, from first-hand experience, what can happen to the innocent just as much as the guilty. Besides that, do you really want to be caught up in such a scandal? As for the family, scandal is the least of your problems, especially as your social circles may change depending on your luck in the world of actual work and employment."

A deathly-pale Charlotte whispered, "This will ruin the family. It will ruin me. There is no way we can agree to this, Ruby."

Edgar looked at his sister and said, "I know, Charlotte. But think of it. It's that or the gallows for me."

Turning to Ruby, he asked, "What would we actually tell the police if we were to follow your plan?"

"I am not pleased with the pain this will cause Leslie Dashwood's family, but I suggest the following. We tell the police that Leslie confessed to us that he killed Granville over a love triangle."

"What love triangle do you suggest, Ruby?" asked Ian.

Ruby smiled. "If Julia is amenable, the story runs as follows. Julia had a dalliance with Granville, though she was seeing Leslie. Leslie found out about the affair and killed Granville in a jealous rage. In a fit of remorse over killing his best friend and political affiliate, he then committed suicide. Or at least that is what we all believe, since he confessed but did not leave a suicide note. I suggest Julia for the role because I believe whatever does get out at the inquest to the newspapers will be publicity for her career. What do you say to this, Julia?"

She sighed, twisted her mouth in thought, and then looked at Ian. He sagely nodded his head. Julia let out a puff of air in exhalation. "I'll do it," she said. "Especially if it gets Edgar out of the dock. As far as I'm concerned, Leslie deserved everything he got."

The Countess looked every inch the fighter now. "Miss Dove, I am grateful for your proposal, but you can quite understand how the conditions are ones that must be discussed in a family conference, which I believe we should have in private."

Ruby shook her head. "I'm afraid not, Lady Snittlegarth. How do we have any assurances that the family won't conspire against us with another concocted story to the police that will implicate one or more of your guests – most likely Fina and myself? The police are due to arrive any minute."

As if on cue, Grimston stepped forward and said, "Miss Dove is correct. Inspector Dolton from the local constabulary rang up ten minutes ago – now that the phone lines have been restored and Lord Snittlegarth had placed the call this morning. They said they would arrive in approximately twenty minutes."

Fina said quietly to the family, "I know you are all in a state of exhaustion and shock, but Ruby's proposal saves Edgar's life, and also saves the Countess and Lady Charlotte from disgrace and possible prison sentences. It is a gift from above. I suggest you agree."

A murmur of agreement arose from the other guests, whispering and urging voices, coaxing members of the family to agree to Ruby's terms. Looking around at one another, the Countess, Earl and Lady Charlotte began to nod at one another. Edgar sat quite still, staring ahead, waiting for his sentence to be pronounced by his family. Charlotte leaned over and squeezed her brother's shoulders. She put her head down on his shoulder and whispered, "It's going to be all right, Eddie... we'll take care of you."

It was not a moment too soon, thought Fina.

They could hear footsteps approaching, insistent and urgent.

BONUS MATERIAL

The Mystery of Ruby's Port

Creating relationships with my readers provides fuel for the mystery-writing fire. To keep that going, I would love to keep in touch with you through occasional updates (no spam) via email.

As a thank-you for signing up, I'll send you **bonus** material that you'll want to read before reading the next book in the series, *The Mystery of Ruby's Port* (to be released in spring 2018).

Sign up at rosedonovan.com for bonus material and newsletter.

ENJOYED RUBY'S SUGAR?

The Mystery of Ruby's Sugar is the first book in the Ruby Dove Mystery series. I'm looking to you, dear reader, to share your views about this series. Reviews online are wonderful and word of mouth is even better.

If you enjoyed this book, I would be grateful if you left a review on amazon so others can sink their teeth into the adventures of Ruby and Fina.

Thank you!

ABOUT THE AUTHOR

Rose Donovan is a lifelong devotee of cozy mysteries. *The Mystery of Ruby's Sugar* is her first foray into fiction, though she has written numerous non-fiction articles, unraveling the mysteries of politics and injustice. Her next book in the series, *The Mystery of Ruby's Port,* will be in spring 2018. Check out www.rosedonovan.com. Feel free to send her an email at rose@rosedonovan.com.

www.rosedonovan.com
rose@rosedonovan.com

GRATITUDE

Ruby and Fina walked into my life with the love and support of so many people. Seva encouraged me to write, even when I was too afraid to show him my meanderings. My mom loved Ruby and Fina from the first read. She provided detailed and thoughtful feedback along the way. Angelique expressed delight in my creative wanderings away from academic writing. Carrie O'Grady, my editor, held my hand gently but firmly through the learning process of tying up mystery plot lines. My dad, Baba, Ben, LaVonne, Randy, and Tania all supported me—even when they were surprised to learn I wrote fiction! My organizing family made me see how it might be possible to combine organizing and creativity. And finally, my cat, Maddie, provided the ultimate guide to being cozy.

Made in the
USA
Columbia, SC